P9-EME-475

NAKED MOLE RAT SAVES the WORLD

ALSO BY KAREN RIVERS

The Girl in the Well Is Me

Love, Ish

A Possibility of Whales

NAKED MOLE RAT SAVES the WORLD

Karen Rivers

Algonquin Young Readers 2019

Published by
Algonquin Young Readers
an imprint of Algonquin Books of Chapel Hill
Post Office Box 2225
Chapel Hill, North Carolina 27515-2225

a division of
Workman Publishing
225 Varick Street
New York, New York 10014

Printed in the United States of America.
Published simultaneously in Canada
by Thomas Allen & Son Limited.
Design by Carla Weise.

The author gratefully acknowledges the support
of the British Columbia Arts Council.

LIBRARY OF CONGRESS
CATALOGING-IN-PUBLICATION DATA

Names: Rivers, Karen, 1970- author.
Title: Naked mole rat saves the world / Karen Rivers.
Description: First edition. | Chapel Hill, North Carolina :
Algonquin Young Readers, 2019. |
Summary: Told from two viewpoints, Kit has an odd, stress-induced reaction when she witnesses her best friend's public humiliation, and the secrets both girls keep may tear them apart.
Identifiers: LCCN 2019015829 | ISBN 9781616207243 (hardcover : alk. paper)
Subjects: | CYAC: Anxiety—Fiction. | Secrets—Fiction. | Baldness—Fiction. | Best friends—Fiction. | Friendship—Fiction. | Middle schools—Fiction. | Schools—Fiction.
Classification: LCC PZ7.R5224 Nak 2019 | DDC [Fic]—dc23
LC record available at https://lccn.loc.gov/2019015829

10 9 8 7 6 5 4 3 2 1
First Edition

For all the anxious heroes, especially L. and L.:
One day, you'll realize just how amazing you are.

NAKED MOLE RAT SAVES the WORLD

Keep It Together

KIT'S MOM HAD A TATTOO THAT WOUND AROUND HER LEFT WRIST. The ink was faded like something that had been washed so many times it had gotten thin and holey and was now just a blurry memory of black.

If you looked closely at the tattoo, you could see that the leafy, twining ink wound its way around three tiny, fancy letters—*k* and *i* and *t*—which stood for *k*eep *i*t *t*ogether. It also spelled kit's name, which was kit, not Kit, because when kit was a baby, her mom said she was much too small for capital letters. Back then she fit inside her mom's two hands, a funny wrinkled thing that looked not-quite-ready to be alive, more like a hairless baby animal than a human being.

"My little naked mole rat," her mom would say every time she saw the first photo ever taken of kit, which had been stuck on the fridge for most of kit's life. Then she would put her hand on her heart.

One day, kit took the picture down and slipped it into a drawer and her mom didn't say it as much anymore, which was good because it didn't exactly feel like a compliment.

Kit's mom had had the tattoo for years before kit existed at all.

"Because I knew you were coming," she said.

Kit's mom often told people that she was searching for kit for her whole life and the tattoo was the map that she followed to find her. She said that when she found kit, she was saved.

Found made it sound to kit like she was not someone who was *born,* but instead someone who just appeared, maybe in a box on the doorstep. Even though kit knew this wasn't true, she sometimes dreamed of scraping her fingernails against cardboard walls, scrabbling to get out.

She also thought that being responsible for *saving* her mom was an awful lot of pressure. Not that she'd ever say anything; she knew her mom loved that story and the way she told it made kit feel things she didn't usually feel. It made her feel *heroic* and kit normally had a pretty hard time imagining that she'd ever be able to save anyone from anything. She was too small to be a hero.

She could still sometimes fit into clothes labeled 6x. That's how small.

"The size in your shirt should be the same as your age," Clem told her once when they were shopping at the Brooklyn Flea, which was the best place in the world to find stuff you didn't know you needed, and kit had felt worse than if Clem had reached over and punched her right in the nose.

Clem was also small, but not nearly as small as kit. She was normal-small. Like kit, Clem and her twin brother, Jorge, had been born too early. But unlike kit, the only fallout for them was that Clem had super bad allergies and Jorge had had to wear glasses since the age of two.

Small-*ish* and *small* were two different things.

That was the day kit had bought her favorite hoodie, the black one with the small rainbow star on the front and the bigger rainbow star on the back. The color was as faded as kit's mom's tattoo. It had cost $5, which was the exact amount their moms gave them each to spend. "That looks . . . comfortable," Clem observed, but she meant, "That looks old."

Kit didn't care that Clem didn't like it. It was big and soft and as soon as she saw it, it looked like it belonged to her. It was already familiar. The fact that it was way too big only meant she wouldn't grow out of it anytime soon.

Clem had spent her $5 on a small glass turtle. "It's not a very turtle-y turtle," she said. "Don't be such a turtle!" she told it.

A lot of what Clem said didn't make sense, but it was funny anyway or maybe it was just funny *because* it didn't make sense. They had both laughed so hard that they had to sit down, right there on the pavement, the crowd parting around them. Clem clutched the non-turtle-y turtle, tears running down their cheeks, while Jorge looked dreamily off into the distance, not quite paying attention to what was so funny. Jorge was like that. There, but not always entirely *there.*

"He has a rich inner life," Clem said, which made kit picture a whole miniature world existing inside Jorge. "But his outer life needs work."

Then she laughed.

Clem was someone who was almost always laughing, at least back then. At first, kit had been friends with

Jorge because she was friends with Jackson and Jackson was friends with Jorge. It had been the three of them. Clem had bugged her, with her always-laughing *thing*. But after not very long, kit started to find the same things funny that Clem did, and soon kit and Clem were the closest friends. Their friendship grew to be the biggest and the best. So even when Jackson and Jorge were busy—Jackson with his sports and Jorge with his "rich inner life"—Clem and kit were either together or talking on the phone.

Clem was the most important person in kit's life, other than her mom.

And Clem got it. She understood what kit's mom was like. She knew what kit's *life* was like and that kit had to look out for her mom because her mom had *issues*.

Kit's mom's main issue was that she was afraid. She was scared of cancer and bad guys and fire. She was terrified of traffic and heights and crowds. She was afraid of spiders and germs and blood. The list was pretty long and always growing.

"K.i.t., keep it together," kit would say, and her mom would put on her brave smile and hold up her wrist so that kit could see she was trying.

Sometimes, kit and her mom would go in the bathroom and perform magic over the tub or sink so the oils and "potions" didn't spill anywhere that couldn't be easily cleaned up. They had a whole glass shelf of bottles and jars, labeled with things like BRAVERY and TRUTH or ROSEMARY and SAGE.

Kit's mom owned a hair salon. She was a hairdresser, not a witch, but kit thought her only employee (and her best friend), Samara, might be both. If you didn't know Samara, you'd think she was just a nice, funny person—she loved riddles—but once you got to know her, you'd find out that she also believed in magic the same way kit did. She believed in spells, believed they could give them courage or love or money or luck, believed in the possibility that herbs and oils and words could really and truly fix any problem.

Mostly it seemed to be *luck* that kit's mom was conjuring, but kit thought she should specify whether she wanted *good* luck or *bad*. Everything was either one or the other, if you thought about it.

And anyway, details mattered.

"You're as small as a detail and the details tell the story. *You* are the best story of all," kit's mom liked to say.

"I'm not a *story*!" kit used to always say back, but now that everything had happened, she wasn't sure this was true anymore.

After all, everybody *has* a story, even if the story doesn't feel like a story when you are the one who is living it.

It's only afterward, in the telling, that it becomes the thing it was meant to be all along.

kit

KIT WATCHED CLEM AND JORGE'S EPISODE OF *THE MOST Talented Family in America* alone. Everyone in the Garcia family was an acrobat. They were amazing.

She couldn't watch it in person because it was being filmed in Los Angeles and they lived in Kensington, which was in Brooklyn, which was part of New York City, the greatest city in the world. It was very far away from California.

Kit was more nervous that day than she had ever been in her life. She was probably more nervous than both Clem and Jorge. It was as if she had to be extra nervous so they wouldn't be.

Sometimes she imagined the three of them were connected by lines in the air, like the invisible lines between stars that make constellations. The three of them made a triangular constellation. A constellation of friends.

There used to be four stars in their constellation. Back then, they were a differently shaped constellation, more of a trapezoid.

Jackson Spencer was the fourth star.

But after Jackson did what he did, he was not their fourth friend anymore. He was still—sort of—buddies with Jorge but kit would have nothing to do with him, and so neither would Clem, even though kit never said what he'd done. That's just how it worked with them.

Kit did not miss Jackson very much. At least, that's what she told herself. She saw him every day at school and every day he seemed to change more, to get meaner, which made her miss him even less. She only missed him a *tiny* bit right when she sat down to watch *TMTFIA* because Jackson lived across the street. It would have been nice to be able to call him and say, "Come over! We can watch Clem and Jorge on *The Most Talented Family in America* together!" He could have walked across the street and flopped down on the floor in front of the couch and stuck his stinky feet up on the coffee table while she waved her hand in front of her nose and pretended it was too gross for words. Then she wouldn't have to watch alone, her heart beating like it was a fist, punching her from the inside.

Kit even went so far as to pick up the phone. Then she put it back down. "No way," she said.

She picked up the remote control. The sun was shining in and she put her legs in the sunshine-y spot, which was warm and bright.

She couldn't stop thinking about the thing that Jorge had said before the Garcias had left, which was, "Don't tell Clem, but I sort of have a bad feeling about this, like something terrible is going to happen."

Kit had told him he was wrong, that it was going to be *great*, that they would probably even win. "You'll be famous," she had told him. "And Marina will for sure probably fall in love with you."

Jorge had had a crush on Marina since kindergarten. Marina was *not* in their constellation of friends. Clem couldn't stand Marina because Marina loved mermaids and Clem thought the mermaid thing was bananas. "Bananas" was a word Clem used a lot.

Kit was on the fence about Marina. She admired people who went all in, but Marina was pretty over the top. She *always* wore mermaid colors. She had aquamarine streaks in her hair. She wore a shell necklace with a mermaid pendant. She'd even once gotten detention for drawing a mermaid with a Sharpie on the principal's scooter helmet. Drawing was what connected her to Jorge even though Jorge didn't draw mermaids.

He drew dogs.

"Ha ha," Jorge had said. "Famous. That's funny." Then, "That can't happen, can it?"

Kit had laughed. "Duh! Of course, it could happen. It *will* happen."

"I'm just sort of nervous, I guess."

"*I'm* not nervous," Clem had said, overhearing the last part. "Why would I be? We've done this a million billion kajillion times." She yawned, showing all her teeth. She didn't have any cavities, which was something she was really proud about. Kit had a lot. "Bad tooth enamel," her mom always said. "You must have got it from your dad."

The thing was, kit didn't have a dad. Until recently, her mom had always said her father was the Night Sky. When she was little, she used to write letters and cards to him, addressed to "Dad, the Night Sky, the Universe, XOXOX." Then she and her mom would take them outside and they would let the wind carry them where they needed to go. When they blew away, they looked like a tiny flock of miniature white birds.

"We've never done it on TV. It's different from practicing," Jorge said.

"Is not," said Clem.

Kit had made a face that meant, "I get it! It *is* different!" and "You'll be fine!" Then she'd handed Jorge the vial of good luck serum that Samara had made. It smelled like luck *should* smell: vanilla and maple syrup and roses.

"Am I supposed to drink it?"

"No!" Kit had no idea what else was in it, but what if it was poisonous? She didn't want to kill Jorge. "I think just having it in your pocket is enough."

"Thanks," he said.

Clem rolled her eyes.

Then Clem and Jorge's parents had hustled them into the big black car that was taking them to the airport. They waved through the open window and shouted "Goodbye!" and kit had yelled, "BREAK A LEG!" which meant "good luck" in show business, her mom had told her, and then they were gone.

Kit got up off the couch and went to the kitchen. Everything she did sounded too loud and echoey because she was the only one home. She made a huge bowl of popcorn and sprinkled it with the perfect amount of hot sauce and then added cheese-flavored salt. It was her specialty. Then she took it back to the couch, with a glass of water. She gulped the icy water between salty, spicy handfuls of popcorn, the ice cubes bumping satisfyingly against her teeth. Being nervous made her hungry. And thirsty.

When the familiar opening sequence of the show began, a fly buzzed near kit's ear and she found she couldn't swat at it. She couldn't move. *I am paralyzed with fear,* she thought.

"Duh," she scolded herself in Clem's voice. *"Don't be so dramatic. It will be* fine."

Kit shoved more popcorn into her mouth and made herself watch.

Finally, Mr. G. appeared on the screen. He picked up the microphone just as kit crunched down too hard on a popcorn kernel. Her tongue poked the sharp spot where the kernel stuck to her tooth.

Mr. G. looked very small on the screen, which was strange because he was normally a big, smiley, blustery, yellow umbrella of a person—a person who *flung* his arms around people and *shouted* about everything enthusiastically. He was definitely *not* a trembler, yet the microphone was shaking in his hand. Kit tried not to notice, because if she noticed then that meant other people might also notice and she didn't want other people to get the wrong impression of Mr. G.

"So what brings you here?" said the judge, the one with the huge beard who always looked bored. "What makes *your* family special?"

Kit thought that was kind of a dumb question. The Garcias were special because they were *amazing*. They were gorgeous and nice and smart and funny *and* they were acrobats. For as long as she could remember, kit had been the audience to everything the Garcias did and she couldn't imagine that the rest of the world wouldn't feel the same way as she did, which was *amazed*.

"My family?" Mr. G. looked down at the stage for so long that kit's breathing started to feel funny: staticky and wrong-ish. "Our kids are as bendy as rubber chickens!" He bent his hands and wrists backward, warming up to the crowd. "They're like octopuses, you know how they get out through little holes in fish boats? Like that! My kids fit through the heads of tennis rackets. Without the strings though!" The crowd laughed and applauded. Mr. G.'s voice got louder. "My wife and I met at an audition. It was love at first sight. My wife is Canadian!" He bellowed the "Canadian" so loudly and proudly, it sounded like he was selling the audience the country itself. Someone whooped. "We didn't get jobs, but we did find each other and the rest, as they say, is history! We've been performing together since the kids were babies! And we're so happy to be here on the greatest show on TV!"

He finished with a huge flourish and bowed so deeply that the top of his hair brushed the stage.

The popcorn kernel dislodged just then, and kit started choking. She paused the show while she coughed and gasped. She couldn't catch her breath but her body kept trying. She coughed and coughed. Then the room went funny and gray and the screen started to blur, like she'd taken off her glasses, which she hadn't.

But just when she thought she might have to run downstairs to get her mom, it seemed like her throat opened back up and she could breathe again. If she had died, it would sort of have been Jackson's fault for not being there, for her not *wanting* him to be there. She added it to the list of reasons why she couldn't ever forgive him. Then she cleared her throat a few times and un-paused the show. She had only missed a little bit of the talking.

"What an *incredible* story," the judge with the strong Southern accent was saying. She was wearing what looked like a bikini top under a jacket that seemed to be made from a clear plastic shower curtain. "Really *heartwarming*."

Was it *that* heartwarming? Kit wondered. *Really?* The octopus part or the falling in love part or the not getting the job part or just that Mrs. G. was Canadian?

By then, Mr. G. had positioned himself in the middle of the stage. The lights went down. The spotlight highlighted the sweat gleaming all over his face.

"You've done it a *million kajillion* times," kit said, repeating Clem's words. Her voice was raspy from all the coughing.

From downstairs, she heard a peal of loud laughter, which was her mom's client, Leandra, who was an almost-famous actor. She had been on three episodes of a Netflix show about aliens. Kit was glad Leandra had a loud laugh. The laugh made her feel less alone than she was.

She was alone a lot.

She was alone making the popcorn.

She was alone sitting on the couch.

She was alone watching Mr. G. talk to the judges.

She was alone choking on the popcorn kernel.

She was alone when Mrs. G. cartwheeled into sight and the music ramped up.

She was alone when Jorge and Clem came tumbling into view.

She was alone when the performance reached its dizzying climax.

But the very worst thing was that she was alone at the startlingly abrupt ending to the Garcias' performance—the terrible, unbelievable, horrifying split second when Jorge appeared to *let go* of Clem and she fell and fell and fell and landed with a loud crash that seemed to vibrate the entire TV and lay still on the stage before the screen abruptly went to the *TMTFIA* logo and then cut to ads.

Kit hyperventilated. She knew she shouldn't, but she couldn't help it. (Kit knew all about hyperventilation, which was when you breathed too much. Her mom sometimes hyperventilated and then actually fainted but that was part of her whole *issue*, which all fell under the big umbrella categories of *panic* and *anxiety*, kit's two least favorite words.) Kit wasn't like her mom, at least she hoped not. But she was definitely panicking, that had to be what it was: a panic attack. If she had to describe it to someone, she might say it felt like something thick and terrible swirling in her heart where her blood was meant to be.

The room started to spin and spin and kit tried to tell herself to stop breathing so fast but it was too late. She didn't remember about putting her head between her knees to stop herself from fainting. The room was whirling around so much that kit found she was clinging on to the couch, like it might throw her off. She closed her eyes, but that made it worse, so she opened them, but then she *was* flying off the couch. "Help," she tried to say as she fell. She landed on the floor, on her hands and knees.

But her hands weren't her hands at all.

They were something *else.*

They were very small and very gray and very *wrinkly,* as though she had shrunk but her skin had not.

"This is *not* happening," kit told herself, but it also *was* happening. It didn't make sense.

Nothing made sense.

She felt very small. Her heart was beating so fast that it made her think of the sound when she had dropped a whole bag of dried beans at the top of the stairs and they all hammered down, all the way to the salon door at the bottom.

She tried to scream, but nothing came out of her mouth.

What was *happening*?

She had to get her mom. Her mom *might* know what to do. Or Samara. Samara definitely would. She could cast a spell on whatever this was that was happening and *unhappen* it, almost for sure.

Beside the front door, there was a big mirror. The mirror went to the floor because her mom liked to make sure her entire outfit, head to toe, was perfect before she went downstairs to the salon. She said she couldn't make other people feel beautiful unless she felt beautiful, too, which was funny to kit because her mom was always beautiful. She couldn't look bad if she tried.

But when kit managed to get herself over there and to look in the mirror, she wasn't there.

There was *nothing* there.

kit

KIT COULDN'T SEE *ANYTHING* IN THE MIRROR EXCEPT THE THINGS that were always there: the reflection of the hall table behind her and the row of shoes and boots lined up underneath, as well as the potted plant with the big leaves that looked like elephant ears.

Her vision was *really* blurry. Her glasses must have fallen off when she fell off the couch.

She squeezed her eyes shut and made herself take a deep breath. She tried to understand what happened: She choked. Clem fell. Kit hyperventilated. She got dizzy. She must have fainted. *This* must be what fainting felt like.

It was not what she expected it to be, that was for sure. *No wonder Mom hates it,* she thought. *This sucks.*

Kit stepped closer to the mirror to try and figure out the problem. When she moved, something small at the bottom of the mirror also moved. She had thought it was a shoe. She stepped back, and it moved back, too.

This was a problem.

The moving thing was *her.*

She was as small and gray and terrible as a very blurry but fairly obvious *rodent.*

Kit tried screaming, but the sound that came out of her mouth was more of a squeak, like when you try to scream during a nightmare, which must be what this was.

It was definitely a *very* bad dream.

Kit tried to pinch herself but her arms were too short, like a T-rex's arms, and she was having a hard time seeing them. In real life, she could at least see her own arms when her glasses were off. But not now. The front hall table, where her mom kept her keys and an umbrella and an emergency twenty-dollar bill in a mason jar, towered over her.

I have got *to wake up,* she thought. *Now.*

She moved so close to the mirror that her nose, or the nose of the thing she was, bumped into it, but she still couldn't see herself clearly, which was annoying. She gently nudged the glass and her teeth tapped against it. Her teeth seemed *really* huge and particularly terrible. She shivered.

"Wake up!" she tried to say to herself, but her voice wasn't working.

She *had* to wake up, she remembered, because Clem *fell* and that was the most important thing right now, not this scary dream that felt like it was trapping her inside of itself.

Samara had told her once that if she was having a bad dream, to try to look at her hand. If she could see her hand, she could get the dream back on track. It was called *lucid dreaming.*

Just do it, she commanded herself. *Look at your hand.* She squinted. Her hand looked like a squashed gray leaf, with very wrinkly skin on it. It was the strangest hand she'd ever seen.

Kit brought it closer to her face and really, *really* concentrated as hard as she could, holding her breath.

She *had* to wake up. For Clem.

And then, slowly and fuzzily and dreamily, her hand became her hand again and swam into focus. Her *regular* hand—a smooth, normal hand—on which she'd written with a Sharpie "math p. 201, 1–14" on Thursday, to remind her to do her homework, but then it hadn't washed off all the way yet, even three days later.

She was lying on the hall floor, shivering.

She was really cold. She felt like she was going to die, that's how cold.

Kit opened her mouth and screamed with all the pent-up sound that hadn't been able to come out before. She screamed all the way back to the couch. She screamed for so long and so loudly that her mom came running up the stairs and burst into the room, white-faced and crazy-eyed. She was brandishing her haircutting scissors like a knife.

"Where is he?" she yelled.

"Who?" Kit wrapped the big, fuzzy blanket around her. She rubbed her scalp, which was as smooth and round and bald as it ever was. That was something that she did, like a nervous tic, when she was upset.

She opened her mouth to tell her mom what happened, but then she closed it again. She didn't want her mom to worry. That was sort of her job, stopping her mom's anxiety and panic from showing up. Besides, her mom had already disappeared around the corner. She was looking for something.

Or *someone.*

"COME OUT!" kit's mom yelled.

The TV was showing an ad for toilet paper. A bear strolled into an outhouse, whistling. "Something terrible happened to Clem, Mom," kit said, but her words were all tangled up in her mouth and what came out was probably gibberish.

"Calm down *right* now!" her mom said, coming back into the living room. "That isn't helping!" She looked behind the couch.

"Mom?" said kit. "What are you doing? Why aren't you listening?"

"I'm listening!" Her mom was looking in the big closet at the end of the hall where they stored their winter clothes and the Christmas tree. "I'm also looking . . . "

"It's *Clem,* Mom. There's no one *here.* Clem fell! On the show!"

Her mom didn't answer. Kit could hear the vacuum cleaner closet door being opened and shut—it was very squeaky—and then the shower curtain being flung aside in the bathroom. The TV had already begun showing the next act, as though Clem hadn't just crashed to the stage. Kit wondered how long she'd been out of it. It seemed like she hadn't missed anything, but maybe she had. The camera zoomed in on a chicken sitting on a kid's head. Kit hit PAUSE on the remote. She wanted to get up and go get her mom but her legs felt too wobbly. "MOM!"

Finally, her mom came back into the room. "There's no one here." She dropped the scissors on the table with a clatter and then she started crying.

"I know there isn't," said kit. "Why would there be?" Kit was sort of used to her mom's panic attacks, but sometimes they were a lot to take in. "Don't *cry*."

Her mom took a deep, long, slow, shaky breath. That was how she calmed herself down. There had been a man *wearing a Batman mask* in their neighborhood breaking into apartments, kit's mom then explained. Leandra had just told her. Well, *one* apartment, she amended. "But still," she said. "He wasn't caught."

When kit didn't really react, she added, "He almost scared the woman who lived there to *death*. She came home! She caught him in the act! She said she couldn't even scream, she was paralyzed by fear. He *could* have killed her. He stole her purse and a kitchen clock. What if he'd murdered her?"

The back of kit's neck had prickled. "Paralyzed by fear," she repeated. It was something she didn't say or hear very often, yet here it was *again*. "We don't have a kitchen clock and anyway, I'm not a woman."

Kit knew these things were beside the point, but it seemed important to say them.

"You're a girl," said her mom. "You're a pre-woman."

"Well, I don't look like one."

"You look like a girl," said her mom. "You *are* a girl."

Kit's mouth tried to form the words to tell her mom the actual problem, the *something terrible* that happened to Clem on TV, but it no longer felt real.

Maybe, she thought, *it didn't happen.*

Maybe nothing happened. Maybe Clem and Jorge hadn't even begun yet. Maybe when she choked on the popcorn, she passed out and both things were part of the same bad dream. She brightened up.

"I do not look like a girl." Having this conversation was normal. They had it a lot, every time someone mistook her for a boy. She was fine with their mistake. After all, she knew what she looked like. Her face was mostly hidden by her thick tinted glasses that made her eyes look huge. And she had no hair.

The thing was, she *liked* being bald. She liked the silky feel of the air against her skin. Besides, she'd seen hair under a microscope and she was glad to not have that be a part of her. But mostly she loved what it was called: *alopecia universalis.*

A galaxy, she thought. *The universe.*

It made sense to her especially when she believed her father was the Night Sky. She must have got it from him, like how Clem had got good teeth from her dad, and Jackson had got athleticism and detective skills from his.

The only bad thing about having alopecia universalis was that people assumed that she had cancer. When that happened, kit felt like she'd run right up to a kid who *did* have cancer and ripped something literally right out of his hands. But she didn't wear wigs. They were uncomfortable and felt like floppy lies, slipping around on her scalp. Besides, wigs seemed to kit to have to do with making other people feel better and it wasn't her job to do that.

"You do *so* look like a girl," said kit's mother, sounding irritated, like always. "You're beautiful. Look at your face!"

"Errrrrhmm," kit said, by way of not answering. She pointed at the screen. "Clem," she said. "She *fell*." She let out one huge sob that she hadn't known was there. It surprised both of them.

Her mom looked startled. Kit almost never cried. "What?" she said.

"What is wrong with you?" kit whispered to herself.

"What *is* wrong with me?" Kit's mom leaned on the wall as though she would collapse if it weren't there. "I shouldn't have told you about that man! I'm a terrible mother. What kind of mother tells a ten-year-old something like that?"

Kit shrugged. "I'm *eleven*." It was too late, anyway. The Batman-masked man was real to her now. He may as well have been sitting on the couch next to her, someone's kitchen clock—what was a *kitchen clock*, anyway?—perched on his lap.

"Kit," her mom said, but then she got choked up before she could finish the sentence.

"Mom, *stop*. It's *Clem*. This is about Clem."

Kit rewound and then pressed PLAY, the sound turned down so low she could hear both of their breathing.

There was Mr. G. doing a backflip away from the microphone after he finished speaking. There was Mrs. G. *twirling twirling twirling* and then leaping into his arms and suddenly upside down on his shoulders in the splits.

Then there they were: Clem and Jorge.

They were both smiling so widely that you could see their braces and even the teeth at the very back of their mouths. And their visible skin was covered with glitter that made it shimmer like the shell of the iridescent beetles that showed up in the summer.

They cartwheeled and jumped and flipped and bounced like the stage was made of rubber, which it was not. They climbed their parents as though their parents were a tree, one on each side, then one on each of their mom's legs, and then their mom scissored her legs somehow and they were higher still, Clem on top of Jorge, who was on top of their mom, who was on top of their dad, hands to feet, like a human ladder that reached up and up and up.

Goose bumps appeared on kit's arms and legs.

She felt like she should be able to stop it from happening this time, but she knew she couldn't.

Mr. Garcia climbed on the chair.

He stepped up onto the table and with the three others balanced on his shoulders, he reached behind himself, picked up the chair and put it up on the table, and *climbed onto the chair.*

Kit's mom gasped.

Clem, who was at the top of the human ladder, flipped upright and then back onto her hands while balanced on Jorge, who was balanced on Mrs. Garcia, who was balanced on Mr. Garcia. Mrs. Garcia's arms were quivering just the tiniest bit, kit noticed this time.

The human tower teetered and then miraculously righted itself.

The camera zoomed in on the judges: one was wide-eyed, as if making a joke about being terrified. One was covering her face, peeking out between her fingers. The third one was sipping his Coke and spinning his pen on his finger as though nothing unusual were happening.

Finally, the camera panned the audience. A lot of people were covering their mouths, as if their unmuffled gasps might unbalance the Garcia family.

And then Mr. G. lifted up one leg like a stork and shouted a word that didn't sound like a word, something between an *OOOOOH* and a *HAAAAAAAAH,* the whole wobbly human pile balanced on his broad shoulders. Then he slowly began to spin.

The music got more ominous, as though it knew what was about to happen. Kit knew what was about to happen, too. She cringed and pulled the blanket up around her face.

"Mom," kit said. "This is the bad part."

She knew it was real, but because it was on TV, it also wasn't. Not quite. At least, it didn't feel that way.

Jorge flipped Clem, threw her in the air, so he was holding her hands, not her feet.

They wobbled again.

The camera zoomed in on:

The judges.

The audience.

Mr. G. grimacing with effort.

Mrs. G. with her wide smile, like a synchronized swimmer's, unaware of what was happening.

Jorge biting his lip, frowning.

Clem's eyes widening, her mouth opening.

And then Jorge letting go.

And Clem falling and falling and falling and

LANDING.

Then the screen jumped to the *TMTFIA* logo.

Kit thought she might throw up this time, but she didn't. She pressed PAUSE.

Clem was hurt. Badly.

She had to be.

"Oh my lord," kit's mom said. "Oh no."

Kit's head felt funny, like her brain was buzzing in an inexplicable way.

Something was wrong.

Everything was wrong.

The screen was frozen on the stupid outhouse bear, his mouth stretched into a wide grin.

"This is terrible," said her mom, standing up and sitting down again. "Poor Clem. Poor Jorge. Are you okay? Of course you aren't. How could you be?"

"I am a galaxy," kit said. "I am the universe."

Kit's mom's hand was on her throat, as if she were taking her own pulse. Then she reached over, hugged kit—the long blond waves of her citrus-scented hair blanketed kit's whole upper body—and whispered into kit's ear, "Oh, honey." She pressed her lips against kit's scalp, leaving what kit knew would be a lipstick kiss. "She'll be okay."

Before kit could really explain what she was feeling, which was a *lot* of things, her mom said she had to go back to Leandra, who must be wondering where she was and if she was coming back.

"She probably thought I was abducted by those aliens from her show," kit's mom said.

"Now is not a good time for jokes," said kit. "Can you call Clem's mom? We have to call her. We have to know if Clem is okay."

"Yes," said her mom. She picked up the phone and looked at the piece of paper taped to the wall where they'd written down all their important phone numbers. She dialed.

"It's going straight to voicemail," she whispered. Then she left a message. "Hi, it's Cyn. We've just seen. Please let us know how Clem is, how all of you are." Then she left their number.

Then she walked over and hugged kit again. "I will call again later, I promise. Clem is going to be fine, honey. Breathe." She let go. "Don't forget to lock the door! I'll go as fast as I can. Keep it together, remember? K.i.t." Kit's mom held up her wrist, as though the tattoo contained all the instructions they needed to survive, which, in a way, it did.

"K.i.t., keep it together," kit whispered.

Kit locked *and* bolted the door behind her mom—the Batman guy was still out there, after all—and sat back down. She thought about writing a note that said something along the lines of "No clocks in kitchen" to stick on the front door, so he would skip their apartment. The last thing she was up for dealing with right now was some kind of robbery. But maybe now that he had a clock, he needed other things instead, like a houseplant or a radio. You could never know what you had that someone else might want, that was the problem. Out of the corner of her eye, she could see a shadowy shape that might be a masked man, but when she looked, it had turned itself back into a floor lamp.

Her mom was right. She shouldn't have told kit about the Batman guy.

Her mom often did not quite the right thing.

She also shouldn't have left kit alone. A better mom would have stayed. Kit knew that. A better mom might have guessed that something *more* was wrong. Wouldn't she?

“I hate you,” she said to the picture of her mom that hung over the fireplace. “You don’t understand anything.” Her mom smiled down at her, beautiful and unmoved.

The portrait was an outtake from the photo shoot for the cover of her mom’s rock album, which had been very famous in the ’90s. It had been her only album. When kit saw her mom’s name (her former name, Cyng) mentioned on the internet, it was often with the words *one-hit wonder,* which meant that she was super famous for a split second for one song and then never hit the charts again and disappeared.

Her hit song, “Girls With Wings,” was having a comeback—“a feminist anthem,” that’s what people called it—and her mom seemed even more anxious than usual as though she was afraid someone would find her and *want* something from her. She wasn’t wrong. Kit found a whole webpage devoted to “Where is Cyng now?” but luckily, no one in the group had guessed correctly where they were. She didn’t tell her mom about it, that was for sure.

“No one will find you,” kit said to the picture. “How would they find you?”

But kit knew that someone would eventually figure out that Cyng was now Cynthia Hardison and from there, it wouldn’t be hard to find their address and maybe they would come to the door, but what *would* they want? An autograph? A photo? Her mom always looked camera-ready. There was nothing *really* to worry about. And maybe if it happened, and it wasn't as bad as her mom thought it would be, then maybe she could get past her fear.

"Face your fears!" was what Mom always said to kit. It's just that she didn't always seem to apply that same mantra to herself.

Kit sang a few lines of the song, which was what she did to calm herself down when she felt less-than-calm. That song was woven into kit's DNA. She knew the song was probably why she loved wings, birds, and things that flew; maybe even why she believed her dad was the Night Sky and why it was so important to her that he was.

It all circled back to her mom. Everything did.

Maybe even *the thing that happened.*

The *faint* thing. The *I-turned-into-a-rodent* thing. The maybe-magic thing.

If it really happened.

Kit felt confused and even the memory of what happened was getting away from her somehow, like dreams did. It was starting to feel like something she made up.

She must have.

Besides, if she were going to turn into an animal, it *should* be a bird. That would fit her story much better. If she could be a bird, she could fly up into the night sky and ask her dad for the truth. That would be the kind of weird magic she would appreciate. It would make sense.

It would definitely be a lot less unsettling.

Kit climbed out onto the warm metal of the fire escape and let her legs dangle. She tried to just *be*.

She breathed in lungfuls of the now-darkening blue sky and let the lingering heat of the evening soak into her skin. The air smelled like hot tar and traffic but also like the wilting green of the trees that lined the street. Even though it was September, the weather was still unseasonably hot.

Below her, on the sidewalk, two men were having a loud argument in a language she didn't understand. Their voices rose and fell, angry and jagged. Then abruptly, one of them laughed. While kit watched, the men hugged and slapped each other on the back, their fight completely forgotten. A bus pulled up to the stop and they got on, disappearing from sight. Their laughter was left hanging in the air, a silvery shape that shimmered and then fluttered.

She felt like she was being watched and she also knew that she was.

"Hey, Dad?" she said, looking up at the sky. "Is Clem okay?"

She waited, then a meteor streaked across the sky, just like that. She grinned. "Thanks."

Somewhere down on the street, there was a screech of brakes and some honking. A shout. A dog barking. Some loud music that rose and fell.

Then the sounds of another bus, pulling away from the stop.

It was what it sounded like when life didn't pause, not even for a minute, even though Jorge had been right and *something terrible* had happened.

3 Clem

IN THE HOSPITAL, IT SEEMED REALLY IMPORTANT TO JORGE THAT Clem say what happened, that she remember all the details. His voice made her think of a loud bell, ringing right beside her ear. "Just say what you remember. Like do you remember falling? Do you remember right before? Do you remember going on stage? Do you remember . . . " She tried to focus on him. He kept taking off his glasses and rubbing his eyes and then putting them back on again.

"No," Clem managed to say, which wasn't true, but talking hurt. She tried to shrug, but she couldn't. It hurt, too. Everything hurt. *Breathing* hurt. Anyway, she *did* remember but she didn't *want* to remember. She pushed at him, flapping her arms as much as she could, which wasn't very much at all.

"Are you trying to *hit* me?" he asked. "Why?"

"No," she said again. It was the only word that worked.

The problem was that she remembered exactly what happened. She closed her eyes and replaced Jorge's face with the red-patterned blackness of the backs of her own eyelids.

She remembered being backstage and how she was, after all, really embarrassingly nervous.

She remembered the kid-magician throwing up into his hat and then crying.

She remembered the family who had trained chickens. One of the kids in the chicken family had put his chicken on his head and the chicken had cocked its head at Clem, like a golden retriever.

She remembered that he said, "Don't stare. Staring makes chickens nervous."

She remembered that she said, "What if he poops on your head?"

She remembered that he said, "She's a *girl*, you dummy," like Clem should be able to tell a chicken's gender just by looking. Chickens all looked the same!

"Is she asleep?" she heard Jorge say, like he was very far away. "Why is she making that face?"

"Maybe she has gas," said her dad. "Babies smile when they have gas."

"Verrrry funny," said Jorge.

Clem felt like she was climbing down a ladder of her own memories, but at each rung, there was a little door with another little door behind it: layers of doors that she kept opening, like an advent calendar. Behind every one was something else she didn't really want to remember but couldn't stop seeing.

"No," she said again.

"Do you think she'll remember what happened?" said Jorge. "When she wakes up for real?"

If you can remember, *can you member?* Clem thought, and then she laughed. *I'll member this to tell kit later. Also, what about* demember? *De*membering would basically be remembering and then intentionally forgetting, or maybe more like erasing.

"Demember," she mumbled.

"It's the medication messing with her," she heard her mom say and then the scene changed, like a slideshow behind Clem's closed eyes.

She saw the exact sandwich that she had eaten: crusty bread, avocado, and some kind of spice that made her tongue tingle. It might have been chipotle. The meat was chicken, which seemed wrong to eat in the presence of chickens.

She saw a dog. *A chicken-like dog,* she thought, and laughed again, except the laugh didn't break the surface. She was too far down the ladder, which seemed to have gone underwater but she could still breathe so it was okay. Okay-*ish.*

The golden dog had leaned on her legs, like he had been waiting his whole life to meet her and now that she was there, he could finally relax.

She remembered the weight of him, pushing against her, and she remembered that she patted him, as though she weren't severely allergic to dogs. Her *hand* did it. It wasn't *her.* It had seemed to be acting of its own volition.

"Honey, we are just going to move you down to X-ray," a voice said. It was a soft whispery voice, the voice of someone kind.

"I 'member," Clem said, and the voice squeezed her good leg, the one that didn't hurt. For a second, she opened her eyes and the walls slid away and turned into a hallway and then an elevator. Where were her parents?

Then the Whispery Voice said, "Shhhh," and Clem made herself think about things that weren't scary, like the thick, soft carpeting on the living room floor at home. "Oops, she's going to throw up," someone said, and then she did, half sitting before falling gratefully back into the fog, which smelled bad now, which made her remember the locker room smell of being backstage—"Flop sweat," Jorge had whispered.

She remembered the lights and how unbelievably hot it was.

She remembered the way people fussed over the judges, as though the judges were the show and everyone else was just an extra and not actually the *talent*.

Someone lifted her up and put her down. She tried to focus her eyes, but they wouldn't cooperate and maybe it wasn't important to see clearly right now. It seemed like the Whispery Voice had things under control, and she was so tired. She heard a whirring sound and then she was somehow inside a sound that felt like it was spinning around her. "Hold still," a louder, more robotic voice said.

Clem reached around. The walls were way too close. Her nose was almost touching the ceiling. She sat up and bumped her head.

"Please lie down," said the voice.

And then, just like that, she remembered falling.

She remembered the way that Jorge was holding her hands tightly and then he wasn't.

The fall had taken an eternity, as though she were tumbling through time itself. She had a lot of time to think and flail and reach out and think: *Catch me. Help me. I'm falling.*

But she also had other thoughts, like: *I'm going to die.* And *Please don't let me die.*

She had time to wish she hadn't agreed to be on the show.

She had time to wish that she'd told her parents the truth, that she didn't want to do it, that she didn't even *like* acrobatics.

Her thoughts whirred almost too fast to actually think them.

Why didn't she say no?

She had reached for Jorge's hand, but it wasn't there.

Just because you are good at a thing doesn't mean you have to do the thing!

Her lungs had expelled an explosive *whump* of air as she crashed into the floor, as though they had burst. It actually felt like she herself had exploded, her bones crumpling on impact.

A wave of pain swept through her that made all other thoughts pretty much entirely irrelevant.

"No." Clem blinked her eyes open. Above her, a fluorescent light flickered.

"All done," said the Whispery Voice. "You did really well." That was funny to Clem because she hadn't done anything except lie there.

"No," she said again.

Then the pain pulled her under and she slept and then there was a weird sweet taste at the back of her mouth and Jorge was back, sitting on the side of her bed and saying, "Do you remember now? How about now?" in a way that made her think of when she and kit used to play in the park with the tube you could talk into from one side of the playground and hear on the other side. "Can you hear me now? What about NOW? AND NOW?"

"No," she murmured again and again, falling asleep and waking up, dreams overlapping with reality and reality spilling back into her dreams, all of it overlaid with a pain that wouldn't quit.

She fell over and over and over and over again in her mind. *Whump.*

Doctors came and went and talked importantly about surgery and *options*, and shoes made noises on the hard floor, and people pulled at her eyelids and shone lights right into her brain.

After what felt like a few minutes or maybe hours, Jorge left with their mom and Clem was alone with her dad. Machines beeped. Her body felt familiar and not familiar, as though pain was all she'd ever known, as though pain was who she was now. Then a machine would hiss and the pain would diminish for a few minutes, but when it didn't hurt, she couldn't feel anything.

"Dad," she tried to say.

Her dad was talking, mostly to himself. He was very big on talking without saying much, even at the best of times, and it all wove in and out of her half-sleep, but she had an important question and she needed an answer.

"The Yankees don't even have a chance!" he said.

"Dad," she said again—it really felt like her mouth was full of mothballs, so her words were probably poisonous to moths, and she pictured them falling dead around her bed, all dusty brown wings and sadness—"Why?"

He looked at her and his eyes widened and she knew he was looking around the room for her mom because this was a mom question, not a dad question, but finally he spread his arms—and even his fingers—wide so that it looked like his whole body was shrugging and he said, "Who knows, sweetheart?" and she had felt something small and hard, about the size of her glass turtle, lodging in her throat.

She coughed, but she couldn't dislodge it, and then a nurse came in and changed something in her IV and she fell asleep almost too fast, like falling off a cliff, or, say, from a human ladder. She crashed into a deep sleep.

kit

CLEM'S MOM DIDN'T PHONE BACK THAT NIGHT AND KIT STAYED up all night, worrying, imagining that Clem was dead, sort of like she was trying on the idea in case the worst happened.

"She isn't dead," her mom insisted when kit had left the next morning. "I promise it would have made the news if she died."

Kit hadn't found that very comforting, but she pretended that she believed her mom. "Thanks, Mom," she said. "I know she'll be okay."

But then, luckily, the principal, Mr. Hamish, made an announcement about Clem at school. He used the words "unfortunate accident" and "miracle," his voice crackling and buzzing over the loudspeaker. It sounded like he was talking about something that happened far away in the world, like something on the news, not about *kit's best friend, Clem.* He coughed and it sounded like a dog barking. *Woof woof.*

"Excuse me," he said, and the microphone clicked off.

Clem and Jorge *really* wanted a dog. They were both obsessed with dogs, but they couldn't have one, because of Clem's terrible allergy. That seemed extra tragic to kit, because she volunteered (unofficially) at a shelter and she knew there were a lot of dogs who *really* needed a family. And the Garcias, who would have been the best dog owners of all time, could not have a dog.

"We could just get a hairless dog," Jorge had suggested, the last time they talked about it. "A kit-dog."

"Ha ha, you should totally be a comedian when you grow up," kit had said. Mostly no one joked about her hairlessness, so she didn't actually mind when Clem and Jorge did. It made it seem like less of a weird thing.

"There have to be some dogs that don't have hair," Jorge insisted.

"Maybe," kit allowed, but she'd never seen a hairless dog and she had seen a *lot* of dogs at the shelter.

"I don't want a bald dog. I want a soft-and-loose dog," Clem had said. "With big lovey eyes. The silky kind that chases sticks and saves you from bad guys." Her voice went soft when she said *silky.*

"A hairless dog could save you, too. And chase a stick," Jorge pointed out. "And have lovey eyes." He crossed his eyes at her.

"Not the same," Clem said.

"Soft and loose!" kit had repeated, and they'd both started laughing. Jorge drew on his placemat and ignored them. They'd laughed so hard, they fell over in a heap, right there on the floor at Dal's.

"Get up, you lunatics!" Jorge had said, which had made them laugh even harder.

The loudspeaker crackled on and then off and then on again with a piercing feedback sound that brought kit back to the present, flinching.

"Sorry, technical difficulty," said the principal's voice, then he coughed again.

"Woof," kit repeated.

Next to her, Jackson laughed. Lately, his laugh felt like it was *at* her, not with her. "The dog is barking. Let it out!"

It didn't matter how many times kit had torn up a tiny piece of paper with Jackson's name on it and blown it into the wind, he wouldn't stop making little comments like that. It wasn't quite bullying, but it wasn't *not* bullying either.

It was extra confusing because *she* was the one who was mad at *him* but now it seemed like *he* was mad at *her.* Why? She couldn't figure it out. He didn't need her. He had two new best friends, both boys named Ethan. They always walked down the hall in a group of three that made the Ethans look like Jackson's henchmen.

"Shut up," she whispered. "Seriously. I'm trying to listen."

"Down, girl," Jackson said, like she was a dog.

She blinked. "What?"

"I've just received an update from Clementine Garcia's parents," said Mr. Hamish on the loudspeaker. "And there is *good good good* news." He said it just like that. Three goods.

Clem was going to be fine, *eventually,* the principal said, *probably,* but first she had had some surgery to have her broken leg pinned together. Kit imagined the pins to be like safety pins with beads, like the ones that she and Clem and Jorge had made when they went to summer camp upstate for five days and nights in July. Jackson usually went, too, but this year he hadn't. Kit still had her beaded pin pinned to her pillow.

Mr. Hamish was listing body parts: *leg, arm, ribs, head, finger.* "Counselors are on hand if anyone needs to talk." That was how he closed it, which made it seem like Clem was not going to be okay at all.

It made it seem like Clem was going to die.

Kit opened her mouth to take a deep Samara-style calming breath, but instead she threw up on her desk.

"I *told* you we should have let the dog out," Jackson muttered.

Kit went home from school right away. Her mom stroked her head and held cold, wet washcloths to her skin as though she had a fever and finally, after what felt like a lifetime, the phone rang and it was Mrs. Garcia finally calling back. She said that Clem said to tell kit she was A-OK, plus she was going to get to miss a lot of school, so *neener neener neener.* "Those were the exact words," Mrs. G. told kit's mom. Her voice was so loud that kit could hear her through the receiver, even from where she was sitting. She also said that Clem was on some medication for pain that was making her loopy. "She keeps taking photos of a fork," Mrs. G. said. "She falls asleep clutching a fork. She calls it Forky."

Kit waited for her mom to stop talking and then asked for the phone so that she could speak to Jorge. The first thing he said was that Clem didn't remember.

He said it urgently, in a whisper shout, like it was a secret. "She doesn't remember."

Kit thought she said all the right things about how she knew he didn't mean to let go of Clem, that it was an accident, everyone could see that. He told her about the sandwiches in the green room and how the show was sponsored by Coca Cola, but his parents wouldn't let him drink it because of the caffeine, which made him throw up.

"*I* threw up," she told him. "Not to do with Coke. Because I was freaking out." She had a Coke in front of her even while they were talking, bubbles fizzing on the surface, the ice cracking as it melted. Coke was what her mom always gave her when her stomach was upset.

"Lucky," he said. "That you get to drink it, not about the barf. I have to go now. I'm going to draw on Clem's casts."

"Draw soft-and-loose dogs. Or a turtle. But a non-turtle-y turtle." She laughed.

"I still don't get that. It's not funny," he said, and then he hung up.

Clem

A LOT OF THINGS HAPPENED AFTER THE SHOW AND THE SURGERY and the physiotherapy and the constant, endless stretching Clem had to do to try to stop her tendons from shortening. They shortened anyway, leaving her pinky in a permanent claw. When she looked at that curled-up finger, she was extra aware of the weird glass-like lump of *whatever* inside of her that hadn't gone away. She'd mostly stopped thinking of it as a turtle. The joke about turtles was from *Before* and that was a long time ago, when she was a different Clem.

A funnier, lighter Clem.

A Clem who could laugh until she cried. And did. A lot.

Now she was a darker, more serious Clem.

She didn't laugh very much.

She didn't cry either.

She just felt flat, like all the ups and downs of her old moods had been rolled over by one of those machines they use to flatten the blacktop when they patched potholes on the street.

She felt like maybe *she* was broken, that was the thing.

She had forgotten how to be herself. Instead, she was this flattened version of herself who was mad about everything.

She couldn't remember how not to be mad.

And she definitely couldn't explain that feeling to anyone, so instead of trying, she *pretended* to be normal, and the pretending was harder than the surgeries and the physiotherapy.

More than anything, she wanted kit or Jorge or really *anyone* to say, "Hey, are you *sure* you are okay?"

Because she wasn't okay.

Everything felt *impossible*, like she was swimming upstream but also carrying something ridiculously heavy, like maybe an elephant, on her back.

But no one asked, so she kept pretending, and a whole year went by.

6 kit

A LOT OF THINGS HAD CHANGED IN A YEAR.

Kit was the only one who felt like she was exactly the same, except for the chip in her front tooth from the popcorn kernel. Her mom wanted her to go to the dentist to have it fixed, but kit kept saying, “No, thank you. It’s fine.”

Kit was a tiny bit phobic about dentists.

It worried her, that she was scared.

It made her wonder if she was going to turn out like her mom, basically a prisoner in her own home.

Every time she touched the chip with her tongue, she worried more.

Clem and Jorge, on the other hand, had changed a *lot. Twelve* looked different on the twins than it did on kit. They had shot up in height and changed shape, so that even though they were still Clem and Jorge, it was as if the roles of "Clem" and "Jorge" were being played by different actors than before.

It made kit dizzy, literally.

Sometimes she'd be sitting in class and Clem would roll her eyes at something the teacher said and make a sarcastic comment about it, and kit would feel like Clem was speaking a different language. She would feel like she'd stepped into an elevator, only the elevator car wasn't there, and she fell, far and fast.

"I can't even," Clem would say. "What an idiot."

Clem thought all the teachers were idiots suddenly, even the ones that kit liked.

"Don't be a turtle," kit tried saying once. It was their old joke. But Clem had just looked annoyed, like she didn't remember the turtle thing, and when she finally laughed, her laugh was not her *real* laugh. It was hard, like rocks banging together. Kit could tell she was just playing along to be nice, which made her feel worse than if Clem hadn't laughed at all.

Now when they went to Brooklyn Flea, Clem just wanted to look at spiky bracelets that looked like dog collars. She wanted to buy vintage clothes that were "emo." Kit wasn't even sure she knew what "emo" meant, but she pretended to, because it seemed like she *should* know. Then Clem got her ears pierced in two places. She started wearing black all the time, but not comfortable black like kit's hoodie, more like *fierce* black. She even painted her fingernails black.

"Clem is just going through a phase," kit's mom said. "Lots of girls go through that. *I* did."

"I don't think I'm going to go through that phase," kit told her mom.

"You might. Just give it time."

"I *won't*." It annoyed her that her mom was acting like it was sort of a joke. "I think I know myself."

"Everyone says that," said her mom. "Then everyone goes through a phase."

Kit left the room and slammed the door, then put on headphones so she wouldn't hear her mom if she said, "That's part of the phase!"

One Monday, Clem showed up at school with a purplish sheen on her cheeks and blue lipstick. It made her look dead, but prettily dead, like a zombie in a TV show. When kit said, "Are you wearing makeup?" even though it was obvious Clem was, Clem laughed and touched her face, like she'd only *accidentally* contoured her cheeks.

"You look like you're wearing a costume," kit added.

"Does it look bad? Should I wash it off?" Clem sounded like her old self. Sort of.

"No. You look . . . fine. Just different. You look like . . . " Kit let the sentence fade without finishing it. Clem looked great, she just didn't look like Clem, she looked like someone else entirely, someone way cooler than kit. Kit still looked like a little kid, she thought, while everyone else looked like the "after" version of a YouTube makeup tutorial. They weren't even teenagers yet! "You look like Marina," she finished. "But edgier and not like a mermaid. Better."

"Want me to do yours after school?" Clem sounded so hopeful that kit agreed.

But then kit went home, dizzy, before lunch, so it didn't happen.

Kit went home "sick" seven times before the end of September. She only left when the dizziness nearly knocked her right over and she got scared she might faint and the thing that happened—the weird *dream*, if that's what it was—might happen again.

"It's your fight-or-flight instinct," Samara had explained. "It's adrenaline and it can make you feel dizzy."

"My instinct is just flight, I guess," kit had told her. "I want to fly away from feeling dizzy." Samara had hugged her.

"You'll grow out of it," she'd said, but kit wasn't so sure. Her mom had grown *into* it, after all.

The only good thing was that the dizziness passed as soon as she left school. "Flight" worked.

And *the thing that happened* hadn't happened again.

Yet.

She had actually Googled "turned into a rodent after hyperventilating" and nothing specifically came up, although she did find one site that said that in situations of *extreme stress*, sometimes people hallucinated. That was probably the real explanation. It had to be. It wasn't magic. It was science. Logical, sensible science.

She was pretty sure that explained it, but she couldn't be *totally* sure. That's why she had to leave school so often. That's why she had to go home as soon as the dizziness began.

On days that she left school early, her mom would see her coming in the door of the salon and she'd stop doing what she was doing and walk kit upstairs and unlock the door and press her lips against kit's forehead or scalp and pour her a cold glass of Coke and flash her wrist.

"K.i.t., remember? Do your homework," she'd say. "Or practice for the talent show. And don't forget to lock the door."

Kit's mom was *obsessed* with the talent show.

The talent show at her own middle school was when her mom figured out that she wanted to be a singer. It was the first time she'd sung on stage and realized that she was good at it. She talked about it all the time.

She asked kit every day what she was going to do for her own talent show and every day kit said, "It's going to be a surprise." She knew her mom badly wanted her to sing, and to be really good, and to get a standing ovation and suddenly know her life dream, just like it had happened for her. But kit hoped that by waiting long enough to sign up, she wouldn't have to do anything at all.

She didn't practice.

She couldn't.

She couldn't even imagine anything more painfully awkward or impossible than standing alone in a room and singing. But she said that she would, and then instead, she did absolutely nothing. She sat on the couch and worried, mostly, after carefully locking and dead-bolting the door against any potential Batman-mask-wearing men. Having scoured the local message boards for news about him, she knew that in the last year, there had been six more incidents involving the mask-wearing man (it *had* to be the same man, she knew) stealing a guitar, a slow cooker, a microwave, an Xbox, a PlayStation, and a barbecue—so far. Kit could imagine his apartment, all set up with the things he'd brazenly taken from other people's homes. What she couldn't imagine was why the police hadn't found him yet.

Once, instead of doing nothing, she pushed her sleeves up and picked up the marker that her mom kept beside the phone on the counter. Then she drew wings on her upper arms. She walked over to the mirror and looked at herself. She imagined they were real wings and that she could transform into a bird and fly away from everything here that was scary (dentists, the Batman-mask-wearing thief) or hard to understand (her mom, Clem, Jackson).

She tried to make the magic work, whatever it was that had made her hallucinate being a rodent. Why couldn't she hallucinate being a bird instead?

But it didn't work, even though she stood there for a long time, flapping.

Then, suddenly, she felt embarrassed. What would Clem say if she saw kit now? She went to the bathroom and rubbed soap all over her arms and rinsed them with hot water, as hot as she could stand, until they turned bright red and only a ghost of the wings remained.

"You are so *weird*," she told herself in the mirror. "Seriously, try to be less weird."

Her own weirdness made her feel extra-panicky.

"You're twelve years old. Do you want to be weird forever?"

She stepped into the bathtub and chose a vial of oil. She wanted to do a spell, but she didn't know which one would work, so she just wrote "weird" on a piece of paper, sprinkled it with peppermint oil, which was one of her favorites and smelled like a brisk cold wind. Then she tore it up into tiny pieces and blew it out the window into the alley, which was hot and felt airless that day, like it couldn't even remember what wind was, much less coldness. She sprinkled out a few extra drops for good measure.

In the mirror, her eyes looked huge against her pale face. Maybe Clem was right. Maybe she *did* need makeup. She looked too *round*: round bald head, round eyes, round glasses, round collar on her T-shirt. If she let Clem *contour* her face, would she look less round? "You would just look stupid," she told herself. "Stupid *and* round *and* weird." She inspected her chipped tooth—food sometimes got stuck in it—and then she went and sat on the couch.

Even sitting on the couch didn't feel right since Clem's accident.

When she had asked Samara what kind of magic could make the accident *unhappen*, Samara had not laughed at her, not exactly, but she'd smiled in a way that made kit feel silly. "I can't do that kind of magic," Samara said. "I'm not a real witch."

"Aren't you?" kit had said.

Samara sighed. "No. But I know that belief is the strongest kind of magic. If you believe something, it can be real."

"What about all your spells?" kit had asked.

"I Google," Samara admitted. "Most of them probably don't work, but what if they do?"

"What if they do?" kit had echoed.

The next time she had a chance, she'd Googled "spells to make things unhappen," but everything she got seemed like a joke, or it had ingredients that didn't exist, like "a hair from a unicorn's tail" or "the feather of a dodo." Then she tried "spells to change people back after they've changed." She couldn't think of the right way to word it to find the magic she needed. Or maybe that kind of magic just didn't exist.

When people changed, kit now understood, they did it both gradually and suddenly. One day you realized they were a different person than they used to be, but looking back, you couldn't remember when they were last themselves, you couldn't see the exact moment when they became someone new.

It could happen to any of us, kit thought. *Even me.*

It had happened to Jackson first.

Now it was happening to Clem.

"This is the last time I'm going to watch it," kit told the Boston fern that her mom had hung from the ceiling in a hanger her mom made by knotting string. The plants had been coming by delivery once or twice a week for the last couple of months. It added up to a *lot* of plants. Kit had decided that the plants were good company. They were like very quiet, low-maintenance pets.

The Boston fern didn't answer, obviously. It didn't care, which was the other great thing about plants. They weren't judgmental, like people. They definitely didn't care if you watched the same episode of *The Most Talented Family in America* a million kajillion times.

Maybe that's why her mom liked plants so much, too.

Her mom had largely stopped going outside at all. She said she didn't need to go outside if the outside was inside. The kitchen—the only room with an uncovered window—was beginning to look like a jungle and smell like a greenhouse. Sometimes kit expected a monkey to swing down from one of the bigger trees or a snake to slither out from a vine.

She didn't mind it though. She liked the plants. But that didn't mean she didn't wish her mom would go outside, just once in a while.

Kit walked over and turned on the air conditioner so it would blow right at her—it was still so hot—and then she sat down on the couch.

Behind the TV, a thick, now-always-closed blind kept the light out, as though her mom was also trying to stop the outside world from trying to sneak in. The "outside world" included her fans and the press, who hadn't cared about her for years, but who suddenly cared again. Fame was stalking her, that's how she was acting, kit thought, as though it was ready to pounce. Kit mostly thought that was a crazy idea, but sometimes she wondered if maybe her mom was right. Just yesterday, in the bodega, kit had heard "Girls With Wings" playing on the radio, just like a normal song that wasn't sung by her mom. The man behind the cash register was humming along and smiling. Kit almost told him the truth, but then she didn't because her mom's privacy mattered more than making the bodega man happy to know that

Cyng lived next door. If he knew, would *he* try to climb in the window?

As far as kit could tell, her mom being afraid had started when she had gotten famous, and this new wave of fame was making it all worse and worse.

"It was just stage fright," kit's mom had said, about why she quit. But kit knew it wasn't *only* that, because her mom had stopped singing altogether, and even when the public forgot about her, she didn't stop being afraid.

So even though the stage fright had been her mom's first big fear, somehow—and kit didn't know how this worked exactly—it had spawned all her other fears, too. And then those other fears had become their own thing and the fact she was never on stage anymore didn't stop them from growing and growing

Kit tried to picture everything her mom was afraid of and how it would look if each fear were a star. There would be so many lines connecting this constellation that the dot-to-dot would create something enormous, like a dinosaur.

Not just a dinosaur, the biggest dinosaur. A titanosaur. An *Argentinosaurus*. She happened to know that *Argentinosaurus* was the biggest known dinosaur right now, but she also knew that was always changing as archaeologists found more and more fossils. Maybe they would find an even bigger one and her mom's constellation would grow to form that one, too.

Kit leaned her head back and turned on the TV, clicking the remote until she found the *TMTFIA* recording from that terrible day.

She fast-forwarded to the family who had the dogs, the exact kind of dogs that Clem had been so crazy about. *Soft and loose* dogs. Kit always watched their act. They ended up winning the show.

Even though they were good, there were so many other things on TV that kit would rather watch, but wouldn't let herself watch. Better things! Her favorite show was a documentary about Antarctica that was on Discovery Channel. She had once learned that Antarctic ice was three percent penguin pee. Three percent! She loved knowing that! There was also no light pollution in Antarctica so you could see a million kajillion stars and, by extension, a million kajillion constellations.

But lately, instead of learning new, important facts about Antarctica, every time kit turned on the TV, she watched the Garcias' episode of *TMTFIA* again.

The dogs finished jumping through the hoops, and from outside, she heard a screeching of brakes. Last week, there had been a bad accident—a car hit a pedestrian who was pushing a baby in a stroller—and kit's mom was now extra worried about cars and crosswalks. When kit had left for school that morning—it was only a three-block walk for her—her mom had hugged her too tight and whispered, "Only cross when you're sure, promise me."

Kit had agreed, but her mom had said it two more times, like she didn't trust her. "Promise me, promise me." So kit promised again and again, but the whole way to school, she had felt scared—and being scared made her sad.

She did not *want* to have any stars in her own constellation of fears. She didn't want to have a constellation at all. She wanted her mom to stop spreading her anxiety, like a virus, to kit.

"Or just get *over* it!" she muttered. She would never be mean like that to her mom's face, but sometimes behind her back, she couldn't help it.

On the TV, Mr. G. was walking across the stage.

Kit suddenly felt scared to watch, which made no sense, because she'd watched it so many times.

"I am not scared," she whispered to the picture of her mom. "I'm not you. K.i.t.!"

She *was* scared though. She just didn't know why.

She made herself watch the whole thing, but this time, when it was over, she pressed DELETE.

"Are you sure?" asked the box that popped up on the screen.

"No," she said out loud, but she clicked OK. Then she went out to the fire escape and sat down, dangling her legs.

"The End," she said to the darkening blue sky. She wasn't sure what it was the end of, exactly, but it was definitely the end of something, if only just the end of her year of obsessively watching that one episode of *TMTFIA*.

She felt relieved.

The thing that happened wasn't going to happen again. It had been a year since the first and only time. She was safe from it now. The year between her and *it* happening made it feel safe, anyway.

Thinking that made her feel brave. Braver than she'd felt in a long time.

"You're not my father," she said to the sky. "Jackson told me the truth."

She looked away. She looked down at the road, where real actual people were going about the end of their day, ducking into the bodega for milk or a sandwich, getting on the bus and going home.

Then she looked back up. The sky was dark and velvety. She knew there were places where you could see a million stars, places that weren't wrecked by light pollution, but Kensington was not one of those places.

Her heart felt small and cold and lonely.

She wanted her dad to be the Night Sky.

Who was Jackson to take that away from her?

"Sorry, Dad," she said. "I'm sorry. I didn't mean it." She lay back and focused on the sky until she saw the first star pop through the darkness. It felt like a sign that she was still okay, that her dad was still there, looking out for her, that the thing Jackson had told her was just a cruel lie after all.

7 Clem

"YOUR GRANDFATHER WAS IN A CULT, YOU KNOW," GRANDMA said. She was standing at the counter in her kitchen, pouring Clem and Jorge some homemade juice. She was crazy about juicing. "He died. Drank the Kool-Aid, as they say, except he did it literally. It was poisoned." She announced it so matter-of-factly, in the same voice she would use to say, "Carrot juice is a great source of beta carotene." She put Clem's glass down and reached up and adjusted a picture on the wall. "That was so crooked!" She laughed, but Clem didn't know what was funny, exactly: the juice, her dead grandfather, or the crooked picture.

Clem's mom was like that, too, someone who punctuated sentences with laughter that didn't always seem related to what she'd said.

"That's not *funny*, Grandma," she said. "He died in a *cult*? Like he was *murdered*?"

"Oh, I know it isn't funny!" Grandma sighed. "Your mother is going to be mad I told you. Drink your juice, it's best when it's fresh." Then she laughed again.

"GRANDMA. Seriously, stop laughing!"

"I didn't even notice that I did!"

"Grandpa *died in a cult.* That's what you said. We are going to need more information, please. Like, right now." Clem took a sip of juice. It tasted like sweet, watery dirt. "This is good, Grandma," she lied, trying to make eye contact with Jorge. She kicked him under the table.

"Well, not *Grandpa.* He didn't die in a cult. *He's* in the living room. But my first husband. Beau. He *would* be your grandfather, but seeing as he was only twenty when he died, it's hard to think of him as a grandpa, isn't it?"

"Uh, yeah." Clem nudged Jorge, who still hadn't said anything, not even about the juice. She wondered if he was even listening or if he was daydreaming about Marina.

"Which cult?" asked Jorge. He was idly sorting through a box of Christmas ornaments, putting the broken ones into a bag by his feet. He picked up his juice and looked at it, like he'd only just noticed it was there.

"Jonestown," said Grandma. "It was called the People's Temple. It was very famous."

"I haven't heard of it," said Clem.

"What cults have you heard of?" asked Jorge.

"Good point," said Clem.

"It was one of those cults that was all about making a new society where everyone was equal. On paper, I suppose it sounded like a nice idea. A utopia. Away from the craziness of modern life, the consumerism, the whole . . . " Grandma spread her arms wide, as though she meant to include *everything*, practically knocking over Clem's unfinished juice. " . . . cycle, I suppose."

"Consumerism *is* terrible," said Clem. "Everyone buys too much junk. Mostly from the dollar store."

"It's good that they do," said Jorge, giving her a funny look, so Clem kicked him again. "What?" he said. "It is! It pays the bills!" He threw another ornament into the garbage bag.

"It pays the bills? You sound like an old man," said Clem. "Are you a hundred years old? Those ornaments are going to go into the landfill you know. They'll take like a million years to decompose."

"It was suicide," said Grandma. "They all killed themselves." She suddenly looked worried. "That's *definitely* not appropriate for young people."

"Jeez, Grandma," said Clem. "We're twelve, not *two*. You're okay."

"A lot of famous people have died by suicide," added Jorge, gulping down his juice like it was delicious lemonade. He burped. "We know it happens. Depression is a sickness."

"Duh," said Clem, but inside her heart clanged in her chest like a bell. *She* was depressed. She sort of knew that but she also knew that no one else had noticed. She was good at hiding it, she supposed.

Anyway, she *definitely* didn't want to kill herself.

You could be depressed and not want to die.

Or, apparently, you could want to die and not be depressed.

"Was he depressed?" Clem asked. "Were they *all* depressed?"

"No! Not when I last saw him. He was . . . hopeful. He thought they were going to change the world."

"Right," said Clem, rolling her eyes. "Change the world."

"Why are you rolling your eyes? People can change the world," said Jorge. "Why are you being like that?"

"Like what?"

He shrugged. "Eye-rolly."

Clem couldn't explain but it had something to do with having a grandfather who would have *got* her. He understood that the world was dumb, but unlike her, he didn't just walk around being mad at it, he *did* something. He joined a weird utopian cult! He had big dreams for the world! He got hopeful, not depressed! He probably wouldn't have wanted to buy junk at the dollar store either. Maybe he could have helped her figure out how to be hopeful, too.

She didn't say all that. "I'm not eye-rolly," she said instead.

"Are you *crying*?" asked Jorge.

"No. Jeez." Clem wiped her eyes.

"Oh dear," said Grandma. "Your mother was right."

"Grandma, it's *fine*. I'm not crying or eye-rolly. I'm just *listening* and drinking this juice. I want to hear it. Please." She held her breath and took a gulp of her drink.

"I shouldn't say any more."

"Come *on*, Grandma," Jorge said. "It's seriously worse to tell half the story. Then we have to guess the details and our imaginations are very colorful."

So Grandma told them: It was before Mom was even born. This grandfather—Mom's father—hadn't even *met* Mom. "Well, not *after* she was born," said Grandma. "Arguably he was there when she was started."

"GRANDMA," said Clem. "Seriously? Gross."

"He left pretty much right after we got married. Marriage wasn't for him. I thought he was the love of my life . . . " Her voice trailed off and she touched her face. Clem had noticed that people touch their faces a lot when they don't know what to say.

"Whoa," said Jorge. "He just *left* you? Weren't you *heartbroken*?" That was how he talked now, like an old person's romance novel. "How did you, like, go on?"

Clem snorted.

Grandma smiled. "I *was* heartbroken. But we'd married pretty impulsively! To get him to Canada, you see, so he could avoid the draft. There was a war. It was partly about the war and it was partly just that he didn't really fit in with a society that was all about making and spending money. He said everything was wrong with everything."

"Everything *is* wrong with everything," said Clem. She finished her juice and put her glass down with a flourish.

"Oh, Grandma." Jorge looked like he was about to cry now, too.

Clem punched him in the arm. "Don't," she told him. "So you really only knew this guy for like a month and a half?"

"Yes," Grandma answered. "But he wrote me letters at first from California and then he went to South America with the rest of them, and then . . . " She clapped her hands. "Well, that was that."

"That was *that*?" said Clem.

"Well, yes," said Grandma. Her eyes looked sad, but she wasn't crying. "That was that."

Grandma and Grandpa—the one in the living room, snoring exuberantly, who would never in a million years have joined a *cult*—lived in a huge rent-controlled apartment over a Laundromat. It always smelled like fresh, clean sheets and fabric softener. The sound of the machines working downstairs filled up a bit of the silence that followed Grandma's story, and Grandpa's loud, pillowy snores from the other room filled up the rest. Clem got up and opened the window. She felt like she couldn't breathe.

"So he was Mom's dad?" Jorge asked. "What a jerk."

"He was your mom's *father*," said Grandma. "I wouldn't say he was a dad, would you? I mean a dad is the person who is there for you. So your mom's *dad* is the one making that cacophony on the couch." She tilted her head toward the door.

"Technicality," muttered Clem.

"We were just kids, so he wasn't *really* a jerk. He was brainwashed by that whackadoo with his whole DO YOU WANT ME TO BE YOUR GOD? I WILL BE YOUR GOD nonsense. Beau wanted to believe that *someone* knew the answers. He just believed in the wrong person, that's all."

"Kool-Aid is poisonous?" asked Jorge.

"Duh," said Clem. "They obviously *added* poison."

"Oh, that makes more sense."

"*Nothing* makes sense. That's the point." Clem sat back down. She meant more than just drinking the Kool-Aid. She meant the whole world. She meant everything.

For some reason, Clem had thought her mom's biological father had died in some kind of old-timey war, maybe in a plane. She was a little mad that she'd been lied to, sort of, by not being told the whole truth. It was a lie of omission.

"Beau thought you could make up a new way of living and just *do* it, that all of society would follow along." Grandma made that gesture that meant crazy, swirling her finger around her temple. "He was lovely, but he wasn't born in the right time. He was cuckoo. But very good looking!"

"Why didn't Mom want us to know?"

"She thought it would scare you. Is it scaring you?" Grandma looked really worried.

"We aren't *scared*," Clem said, firmly. "I think *everyone* should be happy living in utopia. In a place where, like, it's not all about money. It would be better than here."

"Well," said Grandma. "Utopias are always meant to be perfect, but it *always* goes wrong, because people are involved. People get full of themselves. Then the whole thing derails. Lord knows it's happened many, many times. You give all your money and worldly goods to someone who is selling an idea and by the time you realize you've been swindled, it's too late." Her shoulders dropped, like she was suddenly tired from carrying something heavy.

"Oh," said Clem. It was a lot to take in.

"I'm sorry, Grandma," Jorge added.

"What for?" Grandma touched her cheek again. "It was so long ago. I really hardly knew him."

"He *could* have been the love of your life," Jorge said with such a moony look on his face that Clem reached over and punched him on the arm. "Hey! What is wrong with you?"

"Nothing. What about Grandpa? Isn't he the *great love of your life*?" Clem made a kissy-face.

"Well, of course." Grandma smiled as Grandpa let out a huge snort.

"Seriously?" said Clem.

Grandma ignored the question. She was staring out the window, like she could see something really amazing beyond the library that was across the road. "I think of Beau all the time, yet the person I'm thinking of probably never existed, just the *idea* of him."

Grandma got up, her crisp, wide-legged pants swishing briskly as she walked away. She cleared their empty glasses and then left the room and came back with a big, cardboard box, which she tipped over on the table. A cascade of photos spilled out, pictures of a much younger version of herself and a man who looked pretty much exactly like Clem and Jorge.

The photos gave Clem goose bumps.

"Whoa," said Jorge. "He looks like *me*."

"*And* me," said Clem. "We look the same. He looks like *us*."

"He sure does!" said Grandma. "He was a beautiful man."

"*You* were beautiful, too, Grandma!" Clem said. It was hard to tell the glamorous girl in the photographs was the same person as her grandma. "You look like a movie star!"

Grandma did look beautiful in the photos, but Clem couldn't stop staring at her grandfather, Beau.

He had the same eyebrows and longish nose that Clem and Jorge did. He had the same color hair, worn to his shoulders, just like theirs. He had a smile that looked like it went higher on one side than the other, just like theirs did.

"Every time I look at these, he looks younger." Grandma lifted a photo out of the pile, smiled, put it back down. "So many photos for such a short moment in time . . . " She started staring out the window again.

Jorge held up another photo. "He looks like Mom in this one," he said. "Like a man version of mom."

From the other room, Grandpa sneezed. Grandma jumped. Grandpa had a way of screaming when he sneezed that was as startling as an explosion. "Excuse me!" he yelled, then he started snoring again.

Jorge and Grandma laughed.

Clem didn't. "Bless you," she mumbled. She didn't find sneezes funny. She *couldn't* find them funny anymore, not since what happened on *TMTFIA*.

She squeezed her eyes shut, like that could stop her from thinking about it, which of course, it couldn't. The memory leaked through anyway.

The thing was that Jorge didn't let go of Clem.

He didn't drop her.

Clem *sneezed.*

It was *her* fault that she fell, not his.

She had patted the dog backstage and she knew she was allergic.

Maybe she knew it would happen.

Maybe she wrecked everything on purpose because she didn't want to win.

Maybe this mysterious and dead grandfather would have *got* that.

And if he did, maybe he could have explained it to her.

"Well, let's tidy this up," Grandma said briskly, standing up.

Clem cleared her throat. "I'll help," she said. She started dropping the pictures back into the box, but when Grandma wasn't looking, she slipped one photo into the pocket of her jeans.

If she had asked if she could have the picture, Grandma would for sure have said yes, but she couldn't make her mouth form the words. In the photo, her grandfather was leaning against a Volkswagen beetle. He was half-squinting, half-laughing, like the blinding sun was funny or whoever was taking the photo was too bright to look at directly.

Looking at the photos made Clem feel as though maybe time wasn't linear, but instead it was all stacked up like a deck of cards or, in this case, a pile of pictures, and somehow it was all happening at once. It sort of *was* happening all at once, seeing as it was the first they heard of it. It was the first time it happened for them.

"It's super sad," Jorge said, as they put the last photos into the box and put the lid back on. He patted Grandma's hand.

"It *is* sad," said Grandma. "It's sad and it's not sad. Because if it weren't for him, there would be no you."

"No us?" said Clem.

"Right," said Grandma. "You would be made from different genetic material, so you'd be different people."

"That might not be so bad. Sometimes I don't want to be me." Clem pulled her hair over her face. "I could be someone else and the me who is me would just . . . disappear." She made a *poof* gesture with her hand.

Grandma cocked her head to the side. "Are you okay, Clementine?"

"I'm fine. I was joking! Jeez."

Grandma stood up and walked over to where Clem was sitting. "Stand up," she said.

Clem did, and Grandma hugged her. Grandma wasn't usually much for hugging. "Sorry, Grandma. I don't know why I'm weird." Her voice was muffled against Grandma's shirt. Clem kept herself stiff and didn't allow herself to fall into the hug. If she did, who knows what would have happened?

8 Clem

CLEM FOLLOWED JORGE TO A TABLE IN THE CAFÉ, HOLDING HER cookie balanced on the lid of her hot chocolate, but she wasn't listening to what he was saying. Sometimes lately, it seemed like his voice bounced right out of her ear, without ever quite landing. She squinted at him. With her eyes almost all the way closed, he could *be* her.

Only he was a boy. And he wore glasses. And no makeup.

Other than that, it was like looking in a mirror at a carnival: distorted and kind of creepy. Like looking at herself, but not herself.

Or like looking at her grandfather, Beau.

"Beau," she muttered. "Beau, Beau, Beau." The information about Beau was so new, she felt like she didn't know what to do with it.

" . . . and then Mr. Banks was getting all mad, like, losing it, and making us all run laps around the gym."

Clem tried to tune in to what Jorge was talking about. "Is he the sub with the . . . ?" She pointed at her head.

"Yeah," he said. "Dandruff. And he smells like a vegetable garden but not in a good way."

"Vegetable gardens smell like fertilizer and fertilizer is poop. When do they ever smell good?"

"Good point." Jorge looked toward the counter where Jackson Spencer was sitting on a stool, eating all the muffin samples from the tray that was on top of the bakery case. He waved and Jackson made a hand gesture back that Clem couldn't decipher.

Jackson's uncle owned the café. The four of them used to hang out behind the counter, too, when they were all friends. But now they weren't. Kit wouldn't tell Clem why she was so mad at Jackson, but if kit hated him, then Clem hated him, too.

"I wonder if kit is going to stay mad at Jackson forever," she interrupted.

Jorge shrugged, like he was listening, but he was staring at something on the other side of the room. Clem turned. *Marina.*

"I just wish I knew what it was about," she added. "Why is it a secret? Did you ever ask Jackson?"

"Yeah," said Jorge. "I guess."

Clem felt a lumpy aching in her throat. He was obviously not listening. Lately, it was like he sometimes couldn't even see or hear her.

"Mermaids are lame," Clem muttered, to get Jorge's attention.

"What?" said Jorge.

His crush on Marina annoyed Clem more than literally anything in the world.

"Stop *staring*," she hissed.

She cracked her crooked pinky, which made a satisfying pop but still didn't straighten out.

Marina looked up and Clem realized *she* was the one who was staring now, so she waved. If she were friends with Marina then maybe she would feel lighter, sparklier, more unicorn-y. (Or mermaid-y, as the case may be.) Marina frowned, so Clem turned the wave into a nose scratch. Belatedly she realized it probably looked like she was picking her nose.

She picked up Forky and pressed the tines of it into

her thumb, just hard enough to hurt. Then she held it up so that in the picture, it looked like it was growing out of Marina's tiny, distant head.

"Don't post that on Pictasnap if I'm in it," said Jorge.

"You're just in the background. You're blurry. Here, I'll filter you out even more."

She posted the photo. *#forky,* she tagged it. *#forkhead.*

Through the big front window, Clem could see her dad sweeping the sidewalk in front of One Buck Chuck, which was across the street. He liked it to be completely clean, as if a clean sidewalk was what brought customers in to buy $1 junky toys and $1 off-brand soda and not just the fact that everything was super cheap. He did a little twirl with the broom, as though he knew she was watching. "Do you ever think about how all the money that mom and dad got is basically like *loser* money? It seems like it was more money than if we'd won. Why did we get so much money?"

"Duh," said Jorge. "So we wouldn't sue."

"Who would we sue?" she asked and he laughed, like she was kidding, but she wasn't. Who *would* they sue?

She is the one who sneezed. It was her fault. If she told the show that, would they still have paid them so much? Would her dad have gotten the store? And if they found out now, would they take it all back?

Clem took a small bite of the cookie and chewed, even though swallowing past the lump in her throat seemed impossible. Jackson had now moved his sneakered feet up onto the counter and was leaning back on his stool. She hoped it would tip, but just then Jackson's uncle—who she remembered Jackson hated but couldn't remember why—came from the back and unceremoniously grabbed Jackson's feet and plopped them onto the floor. Jackson flinched a lot more dramatically than he needed to.

"You should ask her before you post a picture of her," Jorge said, looking at his phone. Crumbs flew out of his mouth.

"Don't talk with your mouth full. It's wrecking this cookie for me." She deleted the picture. "I'm not going to *ask* her. Jeez. But I deleted it, are you happy?"

"Yes," said Jorge. He put the whole rest of his cookie in his mouth at once.

When Clem and Jorge worked in the store after school or when their mom sent them to help Grandma with something, their parents gave them money to buy themselves "something" and they always got the same thing: these specific cookies. One day they might get sick of them, but that day was not today.

Clem touched the photo in her pocket to make sure it was still there. It was.

She almost took it out, so she and Jorge could talk about it, but he was still looking moonily at Marina. Clem looked out the window again, but watching her dad sweeping the sidewalk made her feel even worse. He was so *depressingly* happy with his dumb store, which was basically a consolation prize for never getting to be an *aerial acrobat,* which is what he'd always wanted to do and didn't. He wouldn't even have the store if Clem weren't a liar. She blinked. She didn't want to *cry.*

A lady with a huge blue umbrella approached and stood by the door to One Buck Chuck and waited while Clem's dad held the door open for her. He bowed.

Clem recognized her, even from across the street.

She pointed. "Mrs. You're-Violating-Child-Labor-Laws," she told Jorge.

Jorge looked. He made a face. "What a weirdo."

"But she's right!" Clem said. "It's illegal for a minor to work after seven p.m. during the school year."

"Is it?" Jackson was wiping the table next to theirs. He swept the crumbs onto the floor and then stepped on them. "That's awesome. I'm gonna tell my uncle."

"Please don't talk to us," said Clem.

"I *hate* working here," said Jackson. "It totally sucks." Jackson swung the cloth onto his shoulder, flicking it into her face.

"Hey!"

"Sorry," he said, but he didn't look sorry.

"So do you think I should tell Marina that I like her?" Jorge asked, when Jackson was gone.

Clem shook her head, no. "If you tell her that you like her, you're going to have to ask her out. Do you even know how to go on a date?"

"No, do you?"

"We're *twelve*. We don't *go on dates*."

"I don't know why you don't like her."

"I *do* like her. She's great. She's . . . Oh, I don't know. Maybe I don't like her. Why do *you* like her?"

Jorge blushed. "She's pretty."

"*Lame*," said Clem. "There is more to girls than just being pretty."

"I know! I'm not like that!"

"Whatever, Shallow McShallowperson."

"I'm not shallow. She's also *smart*. And she's popular, so I'm not the only one who thinks she's okay."

"Being popular doesn't mean anything. It's random. Why do all the popular girls have names that start with an M?" The five most popular girls in their grade were Marina, Maggie, Madeline, Matilda, and Martine. Martine was French, so her name was pronounced Marteen. "I could change my name. Mentine. Men*teen*.

Ment. Menty? Mento. Clem sounds like something that should be in soup. Clem chowder."

"Isn't a Mento a chewy mint?"

"Is it?"

"Yeah, you put them in Diet Coke and they explode."

"Oh, those. I forgot. That has an *s* though. Mento*s*."

"Whatever, Mento."

Clem laughed. She liked how weird it sounded. "I like it," she said.

"You know what, Mento? I'm going to ask Marina to hang out." Jorge grinned. "I'm just going to do it. What's the worst that can happen?"

"She could say no." A wave of mad-sadness swept over Clem like a Diet Coke and Mentos explosion. "She probably doesn't like you. And Mom and Dad would *never* let you date in a million years. You're twelve! What don't you get about that?"

"Whoa," Jorge said. "Okaaaaay. Can you keep your voice down? She's going to hear you." He tapped the table with his pen. "But what if she *does* like me?" He said that last part under his breath.

Without even thinking about it, Clem grabbed Jorge's hot chocolate and poured it onto the table. There wasn't a lot left, so it wasn't as dramatic as she'd imagined.

"What did you do *that* for, Mento?" he said. He was laughing, which made her even madder.

"Because you don't get it!" she shouted, and Marina turned to look at Clem and her face wrinkled up like she'd just seen something disgusting.

Clem pushed her way through the narrow aisle, almost hitting a teenager with pale blue hair with her backpack.

"Sorry," she heard Jorge say behind her. She knew he was probably wiping up the spill. "She's sorry."

"I'm not sorry!" she yelled. She closed her eyes and put her hand on the door and tried to take a deep, calming breath. When she opened them, Jackson was standing right in front of her, so close she could smell his breath, which wasn't good.

She stepped back. "What are you *doing*?"

"Making sure you're okay, I guess. Or kicking you out." He raised his eyebrows all the way into his hair. His face-making was impressive. It was as if his face was made of latex and it could stretch forever.

"That's truly ugly," said Clem.

"Just wait until the talent show."

"*You* wait for the talent show," said Clem.

Jackson looked confused, which was fair enough, because she didn't know what she meant either.

"I will wait. Or maybe I'll invent a time-traveling car and fast forward to it."

"Forget it." Clem rolled her eyes. "I'm not even talking to you." She pulled open the door and cold air rushed in. She didn't want to think *or* talk about the talent show. Why was everyone so obsessed with *talent*?

The wind blew the leaves down the sidewalk in a way that made Clem want to run, so she did, ignoring the clicking in her ankle. The M-named girls probably never did stuff like that, never *ran* for no reason. Clem ran hard even though it hurt all the way up her left leg, which is the one that had had to be pinned. The pain poked at her hip and then up higher, into her side, but she didn't stop, not until she'd run all the way home.

kit

KIT WAS ON THE BUS, GOING TO PICK UP SOME HAIR COLOR from the distributor for her mom's salon. Usually Clem came with her, but when she had asked Clem after school, Clem had said, "No, I have to help Grandma with her Christmas decorations." It was only October, so it sounded sort of like a lie, but kit hoped it wasn't. She didn't know what she'd do if Clem stopped being her friend altogether. It was already terrible that Clem was so unlike herself.

Jackson had always come with her in the past when Clem couldn't, but that was not an option now. She felt mad at Jackson all over again. Why had he had to go and ruin everything?

But kit had to do it. Her mom wouldn't (or couldn't) do this kind of thing anymore, so she bent rules about what kit could (or couldn't) do to make up for it. Last time her mom had done it herself, she'd hyperventilated at the bus stop and fainted and kit knew she'd never do it again. It would always be kit's job from now on, like picking up burgers at Dal's or getting groceries when they needed more than what was at the bodega or picking up prescriptions at Rite Aid, which was not on their block.

Her mom wouldn't go beyond the block, period.

She'd never fainted on their block, kit supposed, but what if she did? What if she fainted in the living room? Then what?

The whole situation was getting a little scary, if kit was being honest. It also was deeply unfair, although sometimes she didn't mind going because it made her feel like she was doing something helpful and important, even *heroic*, although "picking up the new color samples" was probably not quite what her mom was envisioning in her whole tattoo-map-save me story.

So kit went back and forth between feeling like she was having an adventure and feeling like she was being *used* or, worse, enabling her mom somehow. She'd seen an episode of *Dr. Phil* about that one day when she'd gone home from school early and it had stuck in her head. Now she worried about it all the time, along with everything else she worried about, and the worrying made her even more worried.

"Ugh," she said out loud, and she missed Clem so much that her head hurt.

That day, without Clem, it seemed a lot *less* like an adventure and more like a dumb way to get kidnapped—or worse—and kit felt prickly about having to do it. What if something happened to her?

It would be her mom's fault!

Kit pulled her feet up and tucked them under her so she could see better out the window. Rain streaked against the glass on the outside and the inside of the window was getting steamed up because of everyone's breathing.

There were still a lot of stops before the hair-supply place when kit saw him.

He was a normal enough looking man from the back. He was wearing jeans and a black T-shirt. He stood up to let a pregnant lady sit down, which is why kit looked at him in the first place. It was a nice thing to do. But when he turned around, she saw that he was wearing a Batman mask. Kit swallowed a scream, and then she started to choke and feel dizzy. She couldn't catch her breath. She coughed and flailed.

The lady next to kit slapped her on the back until she stopped and could breathe again. "You okay?" she said. "That was quite a spell."

"I'm good, thank you," said kit. Her back hurt from where the lady hit her. She looked at her hands, not sure what she'd see.

They were her hands.

She hadn't turned into a rodent.

Obviously.

Why would she think she had? That was dumb. She was dumb.

"You look too young to be alone," the lady observed. "I wouldn't let you ride this bus alone, no sir."

"Okay," said kit.

"I told you," the Batman guy said. "I'll get you a TV! I promise!" He was using the speaker on his phone and the other person said, "You better."

"Did you hear that?" kit wanted to ask the lady. "It's *him*! He's the guy! The kitchen clock guy!" But the lady would have thought she was nuts. It was so blatant of him to just be out and about with his stupid mask *on*. Was it the only mask he had? Robbing people in a

Batman mask and then wearing it on the bus made it seem like he wanted to be caught. Maybe he did. There was obviously something wrong with him.

"I said I would so I will," the man said. "How big? I can't carry it if it's too big. You know I gotta get it on the bus." He paused. "What am I gonna do, steal a *car*?" Then he laughed and so did the person on the other end of the phone.

Kit's heart stopped beating and then started beating and then stopped again. She wished she had her own phone because she would call 911.

She felt so terrible and dizzy, she didn't know what to do.

Maybe she was going to faint and then no one would be able to pick up the hair color and her mom would lose business and, almost worse than that, kit might start hallucinating again.

"It was just a dream," she said out loud, accidentally.

"That's no dream, that's an idiot who has no manners. Using a speakerphone on the bus," the lady said to kit. "Some people."

Just then, the man in the Batman mask dropped his phone.

He swore.

The phone slid along the floor and stopped right

by kit's foot. She stared at it. She knew she should do something, so she gave it a kick. But she kicked it away from the man instead of toward him.

"What is *wrong* with you, you bald freak?" he asked, pushing past all the standing people to get to his phone. The bus was very full.

"Hey," yelled the lady. "This kid has cancer, be nice. You don't know what he's going through."

"It's *alopecia universalis*," said kit. "It's *not* cancer. And I'm a girl."

"Calling a sick boy a freak," the lady continued loudly. "Who raised you? Wolves?"

The man in the Batman mask tipped back his head. Then he howled. The howl was so big and loud and high-pitched that it felt as though it was coming from inside kit's head. She was so dizzy, she thought she might fall over. Everything seemed to be flashing. She had to get off the bus.

"Excuse me," said kit. "This is my stop. This is where my grandmother lives. I'm going to help her get her Christmas decorations." She didn't know why she added on lies like that. Maybe it was just, in that moment, she thought it would be nicer to be Clem than herself.

She got off through the back doors and took some big gulps of air and then remembered about hyperventilating so she tried to stop by holding her breath. She started to walk but that didn't feel fast enough, so she ran, even though she didn't know if she was running *from* something or running *toward* something. It didn't seem to matter.

She looked at her hands. She wasn't one hundred percent sure, but they did look like they might be smaller, her skin looser.

"This is *not* happening," she said. "Anyway, it was just a hallucination. Science!"

Her body shivered, even though she wasn't cold.

Something twisted hard inside her, somewhere near her heart.

"Not happening," she said. "No way."

But it *was* happening.

The thing that happened was happening again.

"Sorry," she mumbled, squeezing between pedestrians. "Excuse me." Her voice sounded squeaky and all wrong.

This block looked similar enough to her own to make her feel disoriented, as though she should be able to turn around and see the salon and the bodega and Jackson's ugly apartment building and the familiar cracked sidewalk. But instead of a bodega and a hair salon, there was a 7-Eleven and a kids' play place with a huge balloon guy out front. The sign above it said "Play-rama."

"Play-*o*-rama," she said, which would sound better.

Her heart pounded and her mouth was dry. Her brain didn't seem to be working properly but she did know she needed a drink, fast. A kids' play place would have a water fountain, she decided. She didn't have any money for 7-Eleven. She pulled open the door to Play-rama and stepped inside.

"Where's your bracelet?" said a woman. She looked sweaty and frantic. Her shirt said HOSTESS. "You need one." She grabbed kit's wrist and stuck on a bright pink band.

"Thanks," kit said, and then she was in.

The bracelet slipped off her hand. Her wrist was getting smaller. How could that happen? Hallucinations don't shrink your joints. She shoved the bracelet back on.

Whatever was happening was now happening faster, she realized. She didn't have time to look for water, she had to hide.

Of course, she had to hide.

Her whole body pulsed with it. *Hide, hide, hide, hide.* The hide-voice drowned out any other thoughts she might have, even ones about being scared. She *was* scared, but she couldn't worry about that right then.

Kit ducked into a tunnel and began to scramble up and down tubes and ladders, around corners and through narrowing gaps. It might have been fun if she weren't so focused. *Hide, hide, hide, hide.* She wiggled her way into an impossibly small crevice as far up as she could go.

No one was that small, but she was.

At least, she was *now.*

She was smaller and smaller and smaller.

Her dried-beans-falling-down-stairs heartbeat rat-a-tatted through her, woodpecker loud.

She pushed her nose against the plastic, and her teeth clicked against it.

Then a boy's face filled the gap.

He screamed, his mouth wide open, showing a big space where his four front teeth should be. "RAT! RAT! RAT!"

"Look!" she wanted to yell at him. "Don't get hysterical! There are rats everywhere! This is *Brooklyn*!" But she couldn't yell because she couldn't even talk.

She squeezed her eyes shut tightly. She couldn't see much when her eyes were open, just blurs now, but having them closed felt safer.

She started to count.

Counting made it feel like she was somehow in control, which she wasn't.

She could hear the sounds of kids shouting and someone yelling, "Everyone out of the tunnels!" as though there weren't just one rat, but a whole mischief of rats, wreaking havoc in the structure, spreading diseases with tiny spray guns.

She rolled her eyes, or tried to. It didn't exactly work. Her eyes were distinctly not rollable.

A whistle blew, which made her yearn for Mr. Banks's terrible gym class. Even *that* would be better than this. She wished as hard as she could that she was pretty much anywhere but where she was, but nothing changed. Someone banged something against the slide. "Out, rats!" a voice yelled. "Get out of there!"

What good is magic, kit thought, *if it doesn't work when you need it to?*

She counted to ten, then a hundred, then a thousand. When she got to one thousand and one, she noticed that the banging had stopped. No one was shouting. And, most importantly, she couldn't hear her heart quite so loudly.

Her heart felt *normal.*

She looked at her hand.

It was her actual, real hand, with normal-sized skin that wasn't gray.

She exhaled, checked to make sure her glasses had magically reappeared on her face (they had), straightened her clothes as well as she could, and started to crawl, which was harder than it sounds. She'd really got herself wedged in.

When she slid down the exit slide, a staff member who looked not much older than her rolled his eyes. "Did you have fun? You're basically the *only* kid who didn't panic, so good for you. People are such idiots. There are no rats in here. No rat in their right mind would want to be in *this* noisy place."

"I didn't see any rats," said kit.

"Duh, there *are* no rats," he said. "Kids are idiots."

"I'm a kid," kit pointed out.

"Right, sorry." He winked and smiled, showing a mouth full of braces that had a lot of food stuck in them. "You probably aren't an idiot. But you're, like, the exception."

She made her way to the lobby and no one stopped her. She pulled open the heavy door and stepped back onto the sidewalk. It was over. She'd survived it.

Again.

. . .

When she got to the hair place, she gave the girl at the front her mom's account number, like everything was normal, even though her heart was still beating all over the place—*skittering*, really—and the girl went to the back to get the order. When she came back, she was with a man in a suit. He had a huge beard, like Santa, except it was black, and he was wearing a suit with a tie and everything. He looked very official and not even slightly jolly.

He glared at kit and then shook his head. "She sent her *kid*? How old are you?"

"Thirteen," kit lied. Thirteen sounded a lot older than twelve. Thirteen definitely seemed old enough to be running this kind of errand, at least in her estimation. "I'm small for my age," she added. "I have alopecia, not cancer."

The man looked at her over the top of his glasses. They were gold and had tiny diamonds sparkling on the corners. "I like your glasses," she said.

Kit wondered if the man knew her mom, if he missed seeing her and her long blond hair and her wide, slow smile, if he had any idea that she was Cyng. Kit felt like she should apologize for being herself and not her mom, but then the man sighed and said, "Thank you. But tell your mom she can't keep *owing* us." Kit nodded. Then he added, "And tell her you're too little to be wandering around the city alone! Jeez!" He laughed. "You *aren't* thirteen."

"I'm not scared of anything," she told him. "It's fine. I don't mind doing it." *Liar, liar, pants on fire,* she thought. She knew she shouldn't lie, but she couldn't help it. She wasn't herself.

"She shouldn't ask you to," he said. He put his hand out and kit shook it. His hand was warm and soft. He probably had access to a lot of moisturizers or maybe he just conditioned a lot of hair. "Are you okay, kid?"

Kit felt as though if she answered, she'd end up telling him about Play-rama and then about what happened when Clem fell and how she was kind of sure it was real and that she was somehow turning into a rat.

Sometimes.

Maybe only once a year.

But what if it was more than that?

She thought about her wrinkly hand, how loose her skin got.

"Mmm hmmm," she said.

"Pardon?" said the man.

"Nothing!" she said. She suddenly felt like she couldn't breathe. She coughed. "I mean, I'm totally fine. Thank you for asking."

. . .

When kit got home, she put the supplies away in the salon and she didn't tell her mom that she shouldn't have asked kit to go in the first place and she didn't mention the Batman-mask-wearing guy on the bus and she didn't tell her mom what happened to her or that she owed the man money because her mom really didn't need more things to get stressed out about.

She had to protect her mom from all of that.

It was her job.

Maybe that's what made her the hero her mom had been waiting for her whole life. Kit blinked back tears. "It isn't fair," she mumbled.

"What, honey?" said her mom. "I didn't hear you."

"Nothing," kit said.

A couple of months ago, Samara had been sitting with kit on the roof of the hardware store, where they sometimes had picnics. It was a really hot day, kit remembered. The kind of hot where the tar on the roof got sticky to the touch and burned her feet if she stepped on it without her flip-flops. They were sitting on the blanket in the shade of the stairs, eating sandwiches made from sweet pickles and peanut butter on grocery-store white bread that was so soft and light you could roll a piece of it up into a tiny ball and fit the whole thing easily into your mouth.

Then Samara had started to try to explain kit's mom to kit.

"I have to talk to you, to tell you some things about your mom," she said.

It was the first time that kit could remember being really angry with an adult. No one knew kit's mom as well as kit did! *They* were a team. Kit already knew everything there was to know. She understood about the *Argentinosaurus* of her mom's fears. She got it more than Samara did.

"Your mom loves you so much. She's doing the best she can, but right now, she is showing you what she's capable of, and you can't ever expect more from her."

"I know," kit had said. "I *know* her."

Then Samara told kit to stop even *asking* her mom to take her places. She said that kit should take the jar off the kitchen counter where they stored her mom's tips. The jar was labeled DISNEYLAND. That was kit's dream, to go there with her mom, like a normal kid who had a mom who wasn't afraid of everything.

Kit *knew* it was just a fantasy, going to Disneyland, that it would never happen. She got that it was a kid-dream, that it was pretend. But it was important to her to go through the ritual of counting the money and looking for cheap airfare online and seeing how much more they would need.

"It feels like pressure on her," Samara had said. "I know you're a child and you don't really understand, but she can't take that much pressure. I'm worried it's too much."

Kit had been so mad, she'd thrown her sandwich as far as she could. A flock of pigeons had descended on it.

"It's not *pressure*," kit had said.

After that, she hadn't told Samara any jokes for a whole month and when Samara had told them to her, she hadn't laughed.

Now her mom was working with Samara, both of them smiling and chatting while they wove curlers into the long, dark hair of a really pretty girl who was probably a model. "My head is so heavy!" the girl groaned, like she hadn't asked them to do it. "I'm going to die!"

Samara looked at kit and winked. "Hey kit! Joke of the day?"

"I guess," said kit. Things hadn't *quite* gotten back to normal between her and Samara, but they were close to normal. Normal-ish. Besides, she loved Samara, even when she got things wrong and said dumb things, like *she* was the authority on kit's mom, not kit.

"What do you call witches who share an apartment?"

"Um, I don't know."

"Broom-mates!"

"Good one," said kit, even though it wasn't good. "Ha ha," she managed to add.

Samara laughed. "Broom-mates," she repeated. "Who thinks of these things?"

"Great question," said kit.

"Homework?" said her mom, which was shorthand for, "If you have homework, please go do it."

"I'm going, I'm going," said kit.

Upstairs, kit went into the bathroom and looked hard at herself in the mirror to see if she looked any different, but she didn't. She looked exactly the same. She opened the tiny purplish bottle labeled TRUTH. She took a sniff. She wasn't sure what it was, exactly, but it smelled like pine trees.

She dabbed a bit of Truth on her wrists and then she looked in the mirror and asked, "Why is this happening?"

But either Truth didn't know or that's not how it worked because she still didn't have an answer for herself.

At least it smells good, she thought. *If the truth smelled like trees, what would lies smell like?* "Garbage," she said out loud.

She went to the kitchen and found the marker and a piece of paper and she wrote a note. "FYI, THE TV IS BROKEN AND VERY HEAVY." She underlined the VERY and then she taped it to the kitchen window, but in the corner that was mostly hidden by the plants where her mom would have to bend down and really look to notice it. But from the fire escape, the Batman guy wouldn't be able to miss it.

She did not want that terrible man to prove her mom was right to be afraid.

She also knew she was being really childish and sort of stupid—what were the odds of the man coming here, to their top-floor apartment, to steal an old TV?—but she left the note up anyway. Better safe than sorry.

Clem

"CLEMENTINE IS NO LONGER MY NAME," CLEM ANNOUNCED TO her mom, once she had caught her breath from her run home. "Call me Mento."

Mom was making dinner, browning ground meat in a pan. The beef spickled and spat. Clem took a picture for her Pictasnap account. She only ever posted three things: dogs, photos of Forky in weird places, and super-gross-looking food. She had a lot of followers who must have also all been huge weirdos, like her. Who else but a weirdo would specifically like small forks, dogs, and gross food? "*My* people," she thought. They could join her utopian cult. Their leader would be a dog. They would worship Forky. They would only eat food that looked gross.

"Why are you photographing my meat, Minto?" Her mom laughed.

"No reason," Clem lied. "And it's MENTO. Not Minto. MINto would be dumb." She dropped onto a stool and started editing the photo. The meat smelled delicious. It was hard to imagine that it used to be an animal. Cows didn't smell good when they were wandering around in fields or barns. "We should think about being vegetarian. That used to be alive. You know, with feelings and big eyes and a beating heart, stuff like that." She wished she hadn't said that, because now the meat looked too upsetting.

"No way!" Her mom laughed again. "That's bananas! You're a growing girl! Girls who don't eat meat faint all the time."

Clem's mom loved the word "bananas." Pretty much everything was bananas to her. It was her go-to word. Even Clem had started saying it, like it was contagious. Lately, she'd noticed kit using it, too. Soon maybe the whole world would be afflicted by banana-itis.

"How was your day?" Clem asked, just to test her theory.

"Bananas!"

"Ha!" said Clem, but didn't explain why.

"You have to eat meat, Clemmy. Please don't quit on me. Where would you get iron?"

Clem rolled her eyes. "MENTO."

"No offense, honey, but Mento is a terrible name."

"We could eat raisins for iron," Clem said, ignoring the insult. "Lots of raisins."

"That's good, but not enough!"

"I'm *joking*, Mom." Clem took the photo out of her pocket. "Anyway, look."

Her mom stepped away from the noisy pan and peered over the top of her glasses at the photo. "Oh!" She laughed. "My *father*!" The way she laughed before she said, "My *father*!" made it sound like it was the answer to a riddle, like the ones that Samara was always telling. But this wasn't a joke. It for sure wasn't funny. It was her grandfather and he was dead.

"Grandma says he joined a cult and then killed himself," said Clem.

"She *told* you that?"

"Yes, Mom, she did. And guess what? We didn't die! What did you think would happen if we found out? That we'd fall apart?"

"Oh, well. Maybe. I don't know! It's just a lot for a kid to process."

"I'm *processing* just fine." Clem looked at her phone. The meat picture already had 127 likes. "Was he crazy?"

"I think you have to be careful of that word, honey." Her mom pushed her hair behind her ears. "People always have all kinds of things going on. *Crazy* is a pretty powerful word. It doesn't take into account . . . "

"MOM."

"I don't think he was crazy, no." She ran her hand through her hair again, making it stick up in about five different directions. "I think he was troubled and vulnerable. I think he thought it would make him happy. But you know what? I think we hardly ever see happiness in the moment. It's something we only see when we look back."

"Gee, that sounds wise, Mom." Clem leaned back, nearly falling off her stool. She wondered if her mom was right. She had been happy before the accident. Did she know it then? She didn't remember ever really thinking "I'm so happy!" that was for sure. But she had been. "Poor Grandma. What if she had been happy? And he took that when he left? That's really mean."

"I don't think it was mean. I think he felt choiceless, and that drinking the Kool-Aid was not just an option but something he had to do because he was commanded to do it. Sometimes life is like that. It doesn't feel like you have a choice, even if you do."

"Whatever," said Clem. "If he'd asked Grandma, she would have commanded him not to!"

Her mom exhaled, blowing her bangs off her forehead. "I can't understand how it happened, really, all those people dying because that man told them to do it." She shook her head.

"He could have said no to drinking poison."

"Maybe," said her mom. "But I think only a few people even tried to refuse or to run away. Everyone drank it. They were brainwashed."

"Then the *leader* was crazy!"

Her mom had stopped stirring the meat and it was starting to burn. She didn't seem to notice. "Or a complicated person who lost sight of what he was doing who was struggling with his mental health. He really did think he was a god. Imagine what that must have felt like."

"He *knew* he wasn't a god. He knew he was, like, taking their money and stuff." Clem sniffed. "Mom, the meat!"

"Oh, it's burning!" Her mom snatched the pan off the stove.

"Crazy is more interesting than boring, at least," said Clem, getting up and opening the window. "I can't breathe! Too much smoke!" She took a picture of the smoking pan.

"Maybe." Her mom scraped the meat out of the pan and into some bubbling red sauce. The pan was a mess. "I know Grandma doesn't like to dwell on it, so please don't ask her too much more about it."

"Okaaaaay," said Clem, but she wasn't sure she could leave it alone. She had a lot of questions. "I don't get why you didn't tell us before. He was *our* grandfather, too. So he, like, belongs to us. Right?"

"You weren't ready."

"I thought he died in an old-timey war. That he was captured by Germans or something."

Her mom made a face. "Wrong generation. Don't they teach you anything in school? Sheesh. If he'd died in a war, it would have been in Vietnam." She plonked the pan into the sink and added some soap and water. "This has to soak, maybe forever." She laughed.

"They don't teach us about *cults*, that's for sure. No one mentions utopia! They leave all the good stuff out."

"Cults involve all kinds of things that aren't appropriate for twelve-year-old brains to absorb." Clem's mom leaned on the counter next to her.

Clem let that sink in. "I know enough. I know the world is bananas. *Everyone* is bananas."

"Everyone's trying to do the right thing. It's just that sometimes they get it wrong." She turned back to the sink and scraped the spatula on the bottom of the pan. "Maybe we get it wrong and we don't even know we're getting it wrong."

"True," said Clem. "How would you know you were doing the wrong thing if it felt like it was the right thing, the thing that might make you happy?"

"No one is one hundred percent happy all the time, we're all just some fraction of happy."

"Dad is one hundred percent happy," said Clem.

"He loves the store, that's for sure. It's like his calling!" Clem's mom smiled at her. "I like how things are, too. I'm eighty percent happy on a good day. Sometimes even as high as ninety! What about you?"

"Things are okay," Clem said, but that was a lie.

"Give me a percentage, hon."

Clem shrugged. "Happy" felt like something that was a million miles away from where she was, like on a different planet or like a shape she could see only in the distance through thick fog and couldn't possibly get to. "Fifty percent," she said.

"That's low!" said Mom. "Do I need to worry, Clemmy?"

"I'm kidding," said Clem. "Sixty percent." That was a lie. Even fifty seemed like a high estimate. She tried to change the subject. "Abu is another hundred-percenter," she said. "It must come from Dad's side of the family."

Abu was Clem's other grandfather, but he was a completely different type of grandfather than Grandpa, who spent most of his time napping on the couch, or Beau, obviously, who was dead.

Abu was a sparkly, big person, like her dad, but even more so. Kit said he was a *rainbow* of a person, and she was right, he was. He was *exuberantly* joyful. Clem couldn't even imagine him ever being sad.

He designed puppets that he made out of broken things. He had an Etsy shop where he sold them that was pretty famous. And that wasn't even his job! His job was even better than that: He was a set designer for Broadway shows.

Not only was he happy, but up until now, Abu was the most interesting person Clem knew. But strangely now he didn't compare to this *new* grandfather figure who was a dead teenager named Beau who drank the Kool-Aid.

Clem tried to make all that into something she could say out loud, but nothing came out of her mouth. "Sixty percent is probably great for a teenager," she said, instead. "They don't call it teen angst for nothing."

Her mom didn't laugh. "Maybe," she said. "But you're not actually a teenager yet." She still looked worried.

Clem picked up the picture again. "I wonder how happy *he* was."

Clem's mom looked over Clem's shoulder at the photo. "You two look so much like him, in this photo especially. I didn't know him, so I don't know if he was happy, but from what Mom told me, I know he was *impetuous*. You two are a bit impetuous, too."

"Thanks," said Clem, even though it wasn't exactly a compliment.

If they looked like him, maybe they also thought like him. Maybe they were also cuckoo. Bananas. Crazy. Craziness could be genetic, she knew that.

Clem badly wanted *not* to be crazy.

She also wanted him to have not drunk the Kool-Aid, to have become an old man like Abu, a rainbow of a person, the kind of person who definitely would not have killed himself because some crazy person told him to do it.

A one-hundred-percent-happy person.

"I'm going to call kit," Clem announced.

Sometimes talking to kit helped Clem untangle what she was thinking when it felt like she was thinking too many things at once, a woolly colorful tangle of thoughts that she'd never be able to unravel on her own.

That's what she liked best about kit.

Clem

"IF YOU WERE AN ANIMAL," KIT ANSWERED, WITHOUT SAYING hello, "what kind of animal would you be?"

"I don't know," said Clem. "A human? Humans are animals." She thought about the sizzling meat. "Definitely *not* a cow."

"Wouldn't you be a dog? What kind of dog? A *soft-and-loose* dog?"

"I like dogs, but I wouldn't want to *be* one. You can like a thing without wanting to *be* a thing." Clem didn't feel like talking about dogs. She wanted to talk about utopia. She wanted to tell kit about her new, dead, teen-aged grandfather.

"Purebreds are weaker than mixed breeds," said kit. "If you are going to be a dog, be a mutt. I was just at the shelter and that's what Chandra said. Oh, someone adopted Ralphie."

Clem didn't know Chandra, but she had seen a picture of Ralphie, who was basically her dream dog. He looked like a golden retriever, except he was small and had pointy ears. "Oh," she said. She felt weirdly annoyed, like someone had stolen her dog, and then even more annoyed with kit for telling her.

"Chandra says that small dogs live longer, too, so Ralphie will probably live forever."

"Great," said Clem. She didn't want to talk about Chandra, who worked at the shelter, where kit sort of volunteered. Clem had never even met Chandra. She was getting pretty tired of "Chandra says."

"Chandra also says . . . "

"A mixed breed," interrupted Clem. "Small. Like Ralphie. That's what I'd be." She *really* wanted to tell kit about Beau. She was bursting to tell her. She couldn't figure out why she wasn't doing it.

"What percent happy do you think you are?" she asked instead.

"I'd be a lemur," kit said, without answering. "Their eyes look like mine, sort of, with my glasses on. Or maybe a shrimp. Did you know that shrimp's hearts are actually in their head? Hang on." Kit put the phone down with a clunk. Clem could hear that kit was roller-skating around her echoey, empty apartment. She could hear the wheels-on-hardwood sound it made. Her mom had some kind of weird phobia about carpets so all their floors were bare.

Kit didn't have a cell phone—her mom was also super paranoid about brain tumors and stuff—just an old-fashioned phone with a long curly cord that sat on the kitchen counter like you see in old TV shows.

"Honestly, I just wish I were a bird," said kit, coming back, a bit breathless. "Are you still there? If I could transform into a bird, I would be one hundred percent happy, but right now, I guess I'd say seventy-five percent. No, seventy-seven percent."

"I'm here," said Clem impatiently. "That's oddly specific."

"I like sevens," said kit.

"Okay," said Clem. There was a silence where she could have brought up the subject of Beau, but she didn't.

"I feel like I'd *want* to be a bird, but I'd end up being a rodent instead," kit said. "Being a rodent would be gross, right? I mean, it would be the worst of all the possible things."

"You could be a turtle."

Kit giggled. "A non-turtle-y turtle."

Clem wondered if the turtle thing was even funny anymore. She pictured herself and kit as old people, leaning on walkers, rolling down the street to Dal's burger place, howling with laughter because one of them said, "Be a turtle." Instead of feeling happy about that, she felt sort of sorry for her future self, then mad at her current self for only fake-laughing, for not being *fun* anymore, for not even finding the joke funny. She squished the phone between her ear and her shoulder and walked over and picked the glass turtle up from her shelf and pressed it into her cheek. The glass was cool and smooth.

"If you can't be yourself, be a turtle," kit added. "Remember?"

There was a silence. Clem held the turtle up to the light. She could see glass bubbles inside of it.

"Hello?" kit said.

"I found a picture of my grandfather at Grandma's. Not Grandpa, but my actual grandfather," Clem said, even though she wasn't sure she even wanted to talk to kit about it anymore. "We look just like him. He died at Jonestown. That was a cult. It was famous. A lot of people died there. They drank poisoned Kool-Aid." The information came out of her in short bursts, like radio communications in an old war movie, like the kind of war she thought he'd died in.

"*What*?" said kit. She was silent for a minute. "Who? Are you okay?"

"I'm *fine*."

"You had another grandfather who died before you were born?"

"He died before *Mom* was born, even. He didn't even ever see her. He didn't know Grandma was preggo, even. So he was her father, but not her dad. Grandpa was her dad. Because he raised her. He was the one who was there."

"He was her father, but not her dad," kit repeated. "That makes sense."

"I guess."

Neither of them said anything for a minute or two and then kit filled the silence. "Did you know that koalas have humanlike fingerprints? If I were a koala, I'd rob a bank or murder someone and the police would be stumped."

"No, you wouldn't," said Clem. She put the turtle down on the floor and rested her foot on it. She wasn't going to step on it. At least, she didn't think she was.

"Why not?"

"*You* couldn't murder anyone."

"Probably not. But maybe. I could if they were hurting someone I love. Or an animal."

"Jorge . . ." Clem stopped. She was going to say that Jorge hurt *her,* because he did. He *dropped* her. But she sneezed. *It wasn't his fault.* She closed her eyes. "Why are we talking about this?"

"Before you called, I was thinking about something," kit said, "I was thinking . . . " Clem heard kit take a deep breath. "I was thinking that maybe, what if people can turn into animals. Or what if maybe everyone has an animal part to them, that comes out when they're mad or sad or . . . I don't know. Something."

"*Turn into animals?*"

"An animal version of themselves. Like a magic kind of a thing."

Clem sighed. "Kit, come on. We're *twelve.*"

"I know how old we are. Samara believes in magic and she's thirty-three!"

"But that's different. She believes in, like, conjuring up love and junk like that, and you can never prove if it works or doesn't because maybe you'd have fallen in love on that day anyway, even if you hadn't chanted and lit candles and smelled a bay leaf or whatever."

"I was just thinking about it, okay? I was trying to

think about what kind of animal the *best* people would be. Like they would be the most magnificent, right? You'd have to earn that, the magic to become lions or elephants or dolphins. Bad people would have less power, so they'd be crummy animals."

"Marina would be a mermaid."

"Mermaids aren't animals!"

"Fine, whatever," Clem said. "A dolphin."

"Are you mad? You sound mad."

Clem thought about it. She was mad, but not at kit. "I guess I *would* like to be a dog. But you wouldn't get a choice, so I'd be something stupid and insignificant, like a caterpillar or a worm."

"You'd be a mammal, at least."

"No one really has choices. They just think they do."

"True," said kit. "I guess. But this was my hypothetical thing, so I say you get a choice."

"It's just, like, *life,*" Clem went on. "You think you are choosing one thing and you get something else. You don't have any *control.*" She kicked the turtle. It bonked against the floorboard and turned over on its back.

"Right-o," said kit, like it was a joke.

"You'd be a naked mole rat," Clem said. She knew it was something kit's mom used to say about the baby picture that used to be on the fridge, and she knew it really, really upset kit, *and* she knew it was mean that she was repeating it, but she didn't care. She wanted to care, but she didn't.

She heard kit's sharp intake of breath. "Sorry!" Clem said, quickly. "I was kidding!"

There was a bang in her ear.

Kit had hung up the phone.

"Ouch," said Clem. "I hate when you do that." She called back, but kit wasn't picking up and didn't even have voicemail so the phone just rang and rang and rang for what felt like forever.

She felt terrible. She didn't know why she said the things she said sometimes, except she did sort of know. Her mom always said, "Hurt people hurt people." It didn't make sense until you said it out loud and then it did: When you were hurt, it was like you couldn't help hurting the people around you. But she didn't want to hurt the people around her. She especially didn't want to hurt kit. But the scary thing was that it seemed to be happening in spite of how she wanted it not to happen. She pictured her insides being all dark and twisted, like the ancient roots of a tree, scary-looking and gnarly and half-rotten.

Kit's insides were not like that at all. Kit was a great person, inside and out. She would be something *way* better than a naked mole rat. She'd be a *unicorn*.

"Shoot," said Clem. She should have said unicorn, she realized. Kit *was* a unicorn. She was one of a kind.

But anyway, what did it matter? People didn't *turn into* animals. What was kit even talking about? People turned into themselves. Worse and worse versions of themselves.

Like Jackson had. He'd gotten mean.

Like Clem herself had. She'd gotten *dark*.

Clem shuddered. If she transformed, she'd probably be something terrible, like a mosquito or one of those box jellyfish in Australia that would kill you without even meaning to do it, just by brushing by your leg.

She lay down on her bed and curled up into a ball. Her stomach ached.

Once, last summer, kit had brought a whole bag of shining ribbons to the park, and they had found a tree that was just slightly off the path and they had tied ribbons to each branch. On each ribbon, they'd hung a piece of paper that had a wish on it for a person who found it. Like "I wish for you a lifetime of free candy" and "I wish for you a winning lottery ticket" and "I wish for you a puppy named Thor." One of the papers said, "I wish for you that Ben & Jerry's names an ice cream flavor after you." Clem would never have thought of that but it was her favorite one.

Kit was a *nice* person.

She was also a funny person.

But she could also be a sweet person. And a sad person. And a mad person.

The thing with kit was that she was a *normal* person. She didn't have too much of any one quality.

If Clem had said kit was a unicorn, then kit would have listened when she talked about her dead grandfather, Beau, and maybe Clem could have shaken the weird, heavy, suffocating feeling she'd had since finding out.

She tapped kit's number again and listened to the ringing and imagined kit skating faster and faster around the apartment, ricocheting off the furniture, the leaves of all those plants blowing in the whirlwind she created. She hung up when Jorge knocked.

"What?" she said.

"I was coming to see if you're still mad," he said, peering around the doorway like she might throw something at him, which made her *want* to throw something at him.

She picked up a pair of balled up socks and chucked them at the door.

He ducked. "You *are* mad, right?"

"Why do you think I'm mad?"

"I dunno. Because you ran home without me after dumping my hot chocolate on the table?" Jorge had his phone in his hand. He looked at it, then he held it up to her. He grinned. "Marina said yes."

Clem fell back on her bed. "What did you ask her? If she thought you were stupid?"

"Ha ha, no, *Mento.* I asked if she wanted to hang out after school one day at the café."

Clem rolled her eyes. "Don't call me that. I was joking. I wouldn't want to hang out with those M-girls anyway. They have terrible taste in boys."

"You're funny," said Jorge.

"I know."

"I was kidding, you're *not* funny."

"I know that, too." What she had just said to kit was probably the meanest thing she'd ever said. She made room for Jorge on the bed. He lay down so close she could smell his deodorant. He loved this body spray called Axe. It smelled like a commercial for itself. "You stink," she said, resting her head on his shoulder. "Don't wear that on your *date.*"

"You have really good manners," he said. "Maybe you could host a manners YouTube channel."

"Ha ha," she said. "A manners channel. Mento's Manners."

"I thought you said it was a joke."

"It was. So was Mento's Manners. Duh."

"Can you help me pick out what to wear on Friday?"

"No way!" Clem moved over so her head was hanging upside down off the bed. This triggered one of her headaches, which she got pretty regularly since the fall, but she didn't mind this time. She deserved it.

In the first few seconds of a headache, she always saw the *TMTFIA* stage in her mind's eye, the way it rushed up and smashed into her, like she was frozen in place and it was the thing that was moving. Kit had been telling her about a window washer falling off a building. She told the story a lot, ever since Clem fell, like it explained something. And it did, sort of. It made Clem feel better. It made Clem feel understood.

The window washer had survived and so had she.

Kit was a good friend to her and she was a terrible friend to kit and her animal would be poisonous and awful and everyone would hate it.

"Please? I want to look like I'm trying, but not like I'm trying too hard. A hoodie? Jeans? My T-shirt that says I LIKE TURTLES?"

"What is with *turtles*? That's a joke that needs to just . . . die." She made a face.

"You gave it to me!"

"Oh yeah, right." Out of the corner of her eye, Clem could see the upside down glass turtle on the floor. She rolled off the bed and onto the floor so she was eyeballing it directly.

"If you're just going to lie on the floor and be unhelpful, I'm going back to my room," said Jorge.

Clem didn't say anything, so Jorge left. After he was gone, Clem held her breath until she could see stars. Then she did a handstand and stayed that way for five full minutes, just because it felt better to be upside down than the right way up. It was almost as if by being upside down, she was the opposite of herself, which, after all, was much better than being her mean, dark, lumpy, tree-rooty, twisted, jellyfish, right-way-up self.

kit

KIT FOUND THE LETTER HIDDEN INSIDE A FLYER FROM Bed Bath & Beyond.

The flyer had gotten stuck in the mail slot.

Kit took it out because she loved flyers and because she was *really* upset about what Clem had said. She hoped the flyer would distract her, maybe.

"I *wish*," she said out loud.

But nothing could distract her. She knew that. She would probably be hearing Clem's voice saying, "You'd be a naked mole rat," on a forever loop.

Kit looked across the road at Jackson's apartment building. It was four stories and the balconies were all painted olive green. It was a truly ugly building, kit thought. She'd never been inside. Even though they were supposedly such good friends, Jackson had always come to her place. Her mom was sort of his babysitter, she realized. Maybe they were never even really friends at all.

She looked back at the paper on her lap.

The game she played with herself was to imagine what she would buy from the flyer if she had $100. A hundred imaginary dollars. Shopping with this imaginary money usually made her happy. But today she could already tell it wasn't going to work.

It felt like a chore.

She examined everything on the front page and tried not to think the words "You'd be a naked mole rat." The naked mole rat was the elephant in the room. Except it *wasn't* an elephant. It was a naked mole rat. And she wasn't in a room. She was on the front stoop.

Kit thought about the old photo, the one of herself as a baby all wrinkly and weird in her mom's hands. The one that used to be stuck on the fridge. In that photo, she *had* looked like a naked mole rat.

Sort of.

But didn't all new, too-early, wrinkly babies look kind of like naked mole rats?

"My little naked mole rat," kit murmured and put her hand on her heart, like her mom always had when she looked at the photo.

Her mom had meant it as a good thing, but kit had *hated* it. The only one who knew she hated it was Clem.

Clem hadn't meant it as a good thing.

Kit didn't like being mad at Clem but she felt as though she didn't have a choice. She knew she'd forgive her, probably, when Clem asked.

If she asked.

When kit turned the page of the flyer, the first thing that jumped out at her was a rack that heated up your towel while you were in the shower (on sale for $99.99!). Then a pancake pan that imprinted Star Wars characters on your food. Jackson loved Star Wars. "Not that," she said out loud. "Never that." She felt extra mad at him for liking Star Wars and ruining it for her because now she couldn't even consider liking it anymore.

On the next spread, there was a sequinned mermaid pillow, which was interesting, but she dismissed it because mermaids were one hundred percent totally only Marina's thing. Her next choice would be the toaster oven that also broiled steaks and baked pies. It seemed useful and also kind of futuristic.

"Maybe," she said out loud. "Maybe not."

The truth was that if she *did* have $100, she would go to One Buck Chuck and buy one hundred balloons. She'd let Jorge fill them up, because Clem hated blowing up balloons with the helium machine. Then they could run around Kensington handing them out to people who looked like they were having a bad day.

At least, she *would* do that if she were still friends with Clem.

What if Clem didn't say sorry?

She wasn't sure that her friendship with Jorge would stand up without Clem being the bridge. The triangle constellation maybe didn't even exist anymore. Maybe they were just three dots who weren't connected by lines at all, imaginary or otherwise.

Kit turned the second-to-last page, and there, nestled in between a page of plush Egyptian cotton towels in a rainbow of bright colors and a page of vacuum cleaners designed specifically for pet hair removal, was an envelope.

The envelope was light blue and old-fashioned looking. It said "Miss kit Hardison" on the outside. Then it had her building number and the street where she lived. Who would send her a *letter*? The paper was whisper-thin. For a second, she imagined it was an apology letter from Clem, but it wasn't Clem's handwriting.

She tore open the envelope and unfolded the paper carefully. It felt as though she was doing something she shouldn't do. She hunched over so that if anyone were to look at her, they wouldn't be able to read the letter over her shoulder.

"*It wasn't a lie!*" the letter said, in square, purple handwriting. That was all.

Kit sniffed her wrist, which still smelled faintly like Truth. Then she sniffed the letter. It just smelled old.

Kit knew who it was from.

It was from Jackson.

There was no one else who *could* have written it.

There was no one else who *would* have written it.

"What do you *want*?" she asked the piece of paper. "I don't forgive you." But she wasn't sure if he was even asking for forgiveness or if he even cared that they weren't friends anymore. Probably he didn't. He didn't need her. He had the two Ethans.

Her mom had a sign on the wall of the salon that used to be her grandma's. It said, "Sometimes it is better to be happy than to be right." Kit wanted to take a photo of it and send it to Jackson. She wanted to bonk him right on the face with it. What it basically meant was that even if you were right, you didn't have to foist your rightness on other people. You could let it go instead of fighting. You could let the other person believe what they wanted to believe.

"I know he's *right*, okay?" she said out loud. "I know who my father is."

Kit felt the sky start to whirl around her, like a tornado in her mom's favorite old movie, *The Wizard of Oz*, except when she looked up, all the trash was still on the ground where it had been before and she wasn't moving at all. Kit blinked hard, a full-on squished-eye blink. The sky held still again.

Was it happening?

Again?

Now?

"Never again," she said, firmly, as though it was her decision.

There was a time when she *could* have told Jackson what was happening to her, when she *would* have told him. *This must be what loneliness feels like*, she thought. It was terrible.

"*It wasn't a lie!*" she read again.

"So what?" she said. She knew that Jackson had all kinds of "proof." He had photos of her mom with a man. Photos that were taken at a whole bunch of events, exactly eight months before she was born.

He had an article from *People* magazine about her mom and this man.

He had *evidence.*

But it didn't make it the *truth.*

The truth could be bigger and better and more magical than that. It wasn't *her* fault that Jackson didn't get that.

She tilted her head up to the sky, even though it wasn't night, and she said, "Right, Dad?"

Nothing happened.

"Just so you know, I'm okay," she added, which wasn't one hundred percent accurate. It wasn't even one percent accurate. She definitely wasn't okay. Her heart was doing a strange zig-zaggy beat and she knew she was breathing funny, in short, sharp gasps.

Kit wanted to get up so she could show the note to Samara but there was no way to do that without her mom seeing and asking questions and freaking out and besides, she might say that yes, actually, Jackson was right (and obviously he was) and then she would also have to talk about why she made up the whole *thing* about the Night Sky and then kit would have to forgive her for that or be understanding and she didn't want to have to do that.

Not yet.

She wanted it to be her own thing to work out.

It was one thing for her dad to not actually be the Night Sky. It was another thing for him to be *dead*.

Why did Jackson think kit had needed or wanted to know anyway?

What was wrong with him?

He even gave her an obituary for the man—his name was John Alexander Findley—that he'd printed off the internet.

He was a thoughtless *jerk*.

He must have thought kit would say, "Oooh, you're so smart, thank you for being so smart."

He must have thought that she would think he was the best friend ever.

"Wrong!" she said out loud.

Jackson's dad was a policeman. Everyone in his family was a cop: his aunts and his cousins and his grandfather and his uncles. He seemed to think he was a detective, too, like you could inherit it.

"You don't know anything," is what kit had actually said, when he'd presented her with what he found. "You are *so* stupid. I *hate* you."

His face had crumpled up and then he'd stood up straighter and said, "You're the one who is *stupid*, if you really think your dad is the Night Sky. Grow up."

She *hated* him so much then and still, now.

She pressed her face against the note. It *stank*. He probably found the paper in his grandpa's old desk, which he had in his bedroom. It was a real desk from a police station. His dad had had to saw the legs off and then glue them back on again to fit the desk through Jackson's door. Jackson loved that story, he'd told her a million times. He also told her that the desk took up more room than his bed. That did not sound great to kit but Jackson loved that desk so she'd said, "Awesome."

"It wasn't a lie!"

"That is not the point," she said out loud. But it was impossible to explain the difference between facts and magic to a person who believed only in science. And Jackson was that kind of person.

"It wasn't a lie!"

An old man was opening the door of the bodega that shared the stoop with the salon. He gave her a funny look.

Kit folded the note back up and unfolded it again. She felt terrible.

Can kids have heart attacks? she wondered.

She wanted to go upstairs and call Clem, but she was mad at Clem and not being able to call Clem made her feel even madder at Clem, but she didn't want to get *too* mad in case *the thing that happened* happened again.

She creased the note into smaller and smaller squares until it fit into the palm of her hand. She hadn't talked to Jackson for a whole *year.* She never had to talk to him again. But it bugged her how this dumb note was making it seem like she had to *do* something, like it demanded a response.

She looked through the glass of the door and Samara gave her a thumbs-up, like they'd shared a riddle and she thought it was funny, too. Kit wasn't laughing. She was crying.

Jackson wasn't wrong!

Her real father *was* dead!

But that didn't mean her dad wasn't the Night Sky. It couldn't. She might have lost Jackson and she might be losing Clem and her mom might be losing her mind, but kit wasn't going to lose her dad. No way. Not now.

The wind lifted the pages of the Bed Bath & Beyond flyer. It looked like it was waving at her, a pair of colorful wings, but she couldn't pick it up.

A bunch of pigeons flickered—not quite running, but not flying either—on the sidewalk, pecking around the garbage can, which was overflowing. On the other side of the short cement wall, was the entrance to the bodega. A lot of people had gone in and out since kit sat down. The sun had moved to a different place in the sky. The buses had come and gone and come and gone and come and gone. One lady who passed her was holding a baby who was screaming so loudly kit thought he was going to throw up.

No one seemed to notice kit and her impossibly heavy but folded-up-tiny note.

She pulled her hoodie up over her nose and it smelled good, like fresh laundry and the sun. It was still too big but definitely not as big as it had been when she got it. Even *she* was changing, she supposed, just more slowly than other people.

Her legs felt quivery, like when you get too close to the edge of the roof of a building and you look down at the street.

My father, *who I don't* care *about or* know, *is dead*, kit thought.

"My father is dead," kit said. It was true and it was okay. She took a deep breath.

A man wearing a turban was walking by with four tiny poodles all on one leash, three black and one white. They were moving their legs very fast to keep up with him. The man paused, looked over at kit and shrugged. "Sorry, kid," he said. "Mine is, too." He had a cigarette between his lips but it wasn't lit. It looked like a mistake, bouncing there while he spoke.

The poodles yipped. Maybe their father was also dead.

"MY FATHER IS DEAD!" kit yelled.

She hoped Jackson's window was open. She hoped he heard her yelling. She hoped that if he heard her, he would leave her alone again. She was *accepting* it. She *got* it. Was that what he wanted?

The man turned away and started walking again. He had really long legs. The poodles' legs were twinkling, that's how fast they had to move to keep up.

"GOODBYE!" kit shouted, as though suddenly she couldn't be big enough or loud enough to fill the space she needed to fill.

The man waved, but she wasn't talking to him, she was talking to the Night Sky.

As the last dog disappeared around the corner, the

tiniest little bit of lightning forked down from a single cloud that had floated into view. People see what they need to see and kit knew that she needed to see a tiny fork of lightning.

She knew it wasn't real, but maybe it was, and she really didn't understand why the difference mattered.

"I *know*, Dad," she said.

She thought about going upstairs and smearing the note with, say, rose geranium, which was for courage. That's what Samara's list said. The list was printed out and laminated and glued to the tiles in the shower. It would be there forever, even if they stopped believing that lemongrass could clear your mind, even after she went to college and her mom moved to Paris, which had always been her dream before she got too scared to even go as far as, say, Manhattan.

Kit made herself stand up. She opened the salon door, which was super heavy. She felt like she could barely keep hold of it.

She called inside, "Mom? I'm going to the shelter." She tried to make her voice sound as normal as possible.

"Okay, honey," kit's mom said, like nothing was wrong. Her voice sounded squashed but that's because there were hairpins between her lips.

"Mom?"

Kit's mom met kit's eyes in the mirror and made a face, which kit knew meant, "I can't talk now because there are pins in my mouth and/or because this is a very important client." The client was a woman who had very long, shiny silver hair.

"If you're skating, be careful crossing the road!" her mom said, taking the pins out of her mouth. "Go slow!" She leaned toward her client and said, "I worry about her when she roller skates, but at least she can outskate the bad guys!"

Kit immediately pictured herself skating, fast, away from the guy with a Batman mask. "Mom," she said, weakly.

The lady winked.

"Oh Cyn," said Samara. "Don't freak her out! It's only a few blocks."

Samara swooped in for a hug. Kit wanted to stay in the hug forever, breathing in whatever oils Samara was using to ward off bad luck today, but Samara released her, holding her at arm's length. "You're looking taller!"

"Thanks," said kit. "Since this morning?"

"You have to grow sometime!" Samara said. "Maybe you had a growth spurt at noon!"

"Maybe." Kit smiled. "Probably."

"I have a new one for you," said Samara. "Ready?"

"Ready," said kit.

"What did the math book say to the calculator?"

"Ummmmm, I don't know." Kit looked at the door.

"I have a lot of problems!" Samara grinned.

"Me too," said kit.

"That's the answer to the riddle!"

Kit mustered up a laugh. "I get it. That's a good one. I have a lot of problems," she repeated. She *did* have a lot of problems.

"Are you okay?"

"I'm good," kit lied. "I'm fine. Just, you know, growing. Growing is tiring."

"You're almost a teenager. A teenager!" said Samara.

Kit rolled her eyes and Samara went back to rinsing the customer who was at the sinks, and her mom kept snipping. "I saw that eye roll, that's a teenager thing!" she said.

The silver-haired lady met kit's eye and she gave a small nod. The nod said, "I see you."

At least, that's how it felt.

Kit put on her helmet and skated into the bathroom. There was a tiny bottle of clove oil, labeled BRAVERY, beside the sink. She put a tiny dab of it on the inside of her wrist. It completely obliterated the smell of Truth.

She looked in the mirror. Her glasses looked like gray circles over her face. Like a mask.

Almost.

Kit left the salon, sidestepping down the front steps.

She glided around a group of women pushing strollers. She dodged an elderly man dragging a wagon full of groceries. She wove in between two girls who were taking a selfie. "Photobomb," she said.

Chandra, who was seventeen and worked *officially* at the shelter, was literally the *least* likely person kit knew who might *get* some of what was happening, who might have an answer, or even know what the question was. But she was also the only person kit had left to tell.

13 Clem

IT WAS THE FIRST TIME CLEM HAD GONE WITH JORGE TO ONE OF Abu's shows since *The Most Talented Family in America*, and she felt funny about it. Jorge, of course, had never stopped going. He always wanted to help and Abu always asked for help even though they weren't really helpful. Jorge was so *Jorge* sometimes that she wanted to scream.

Specifically, she wanted to scream, "STOP BEING SO HELPFUL!"

An off-Broadway musical wasn't the same thing as a TV talent show, but it also *was* the same thing. It was a *spectacle*. There were the same lights and the same hustle and bustle and the same dusty smell that seemed to always hang around stages (even when they were clean) and the same rows and rows of empty seats in the audience waiting to be filled.

This particular show was taking place at a small theater off-off-off-Broadway. It was not Abu's usual kind of job, which *should* have made it no big deal, but Clem was nervous, all the same. "It's not like you're *in* the show!" she told herself. "Keep it together!"

Keep It Together was a kit-thing, so right away, she felt bad all over again about kit. She dug her fingernails into her arm because for some reason, the pinch of them made her feel better.

"This show is a labor of love for me!" Abu said. "Which means I'm working for almost nothing, but I love this crazy, magnificent show. Sometimes you have to do things just for fun and I'm having a blast!" He high-fived the air.

His exuberance made Clem ache for the person she used to be and wasn't anymore.

Had she ever been that happy about anything? Ever?

"Do you *love* it?" asked Abu. He held his arms out, like he was going to embrace the entire stage.

"It looks good," said Clem. "I like it."

"It's *amazing*, Abu!" Jorge said. "It's *the best*!" He whooped and then ran across the stage, jumped off, and hopped over the rows of seats until he was in the middle of where the audience would be. "IT'S SO GREAT FROM HERE, TOO!" he yelled. He did two thumbs up, which seemed like one too many, to Clem. She scowled. Too much unbridled enthusiasm made her prickly.

"Settle down," she mumbled, but not loudly enough for anyone else to hear.

Sometimes, like now, it felt as though it was her *job* to keep everyone from getting too wildly enthusiastic, too crazily out of control and her job was exhausting. Unbearable, really.

Clem wandered over to the side of the stage, crouched in the wings and looked back at the set. It was definitely *different*. Everything was built to look as though it were being viewed through a twisty, distorted lens. Buildings and trees and huge fire hydrants painted crazy colors that glowed under black lights all hung at different angles, moving slightly like they were in a breeze. The movement made her eyes feel like they couldn't focus, which made her a bit queasy. And, anyway, if she were to be critical, she'd say that the skyline was *too* tall and *too* bendy. The up-close buildings had windows with lumpy rivulets running down them that looked like melting wax. There were feathers and flowers and color everywhere, so much *color.*

Too much color.

Abu crouched down next to her. "How does it look from here?" he said, squinting. "Good, huh?"

"It's making my eyes cross," Clem said, honestly. "It's great, it's just a *lot,*" she added.

"It's sort of like if a paint store threw up," said Abu. "But in a good way, right?"

"It's so *awesome*!" said Jorge, running back up onto the stage. "I think you blew my mind. Where is my mind?" He felt around, like he was blindly looking for it.

"You are *so* weird," said Clem, standing up. Crouching like that was hurting her hip. Abu stood up, too, and Jorge and Abu laughed, so she laughed, too, so she wouldn't be left out.

The show was called *Dogs,* which was why Abu knew the twins would want to come. It was "an homage" to *Cats,* he explained, except it was also a spoof. A spoof was a joke.

Clem wasn't clear how something could honor something else while at the same time making fun of it.

Clem and Jorge were in charge of going next door to pick up a big order of food for the cast and crew, and then after that, they were going to "make themselves scarce" and then, finally, they'd get to watch the show from the wings. Clem had seen so many shows from the side, she had lost count, but only one show from the audience. That show was *Hamilton.* It was the best show she had ever seen in her life but Abu hadn't worked on that one, so they'd had to get regular tickets, which they got to celebrate being chosen to perform on *TMTFIA*. It felt like a lifetime ago, but it was also the last time Clem could remember being even *close* to one hundred percent happy.

Now she knew that they'd been dumb to be so happy about being chosen for the show. Maybe being happy about anything is dumb. *Anything could go wrong,* she thought, *at any time.*

She kicked the leg of a folding chair and it tipped over.

"Hey!" said Jorge. "What did you do that for?" He picked the chair up.

"I didn't. It fell."

"You did *so,* I saw you."

"You don't know everything that you think you know." The dark, buzzing feeling was swarming all over her again, like black flies. She wanted to yell, "HELP!" but she also wanted to cry. She wanted Jorge to notice but she also wanted him to go away. "Go away," she said, finally.

"Fine, weirdo."

"Takes one to know one," she said back, which was stupid because what she'd meant was, "I'm not okay. Can you help me?"

But she didn't say that.

Kit had always said that the three of them made a constellation, but now they were all three just completely separate stars, disconnected, but banging into each other every once in a while, making black holes in the universe that made everything good disappear.

The theater hummed with the usual last-minute preparations.

The actors were warming up, the set was being adjusted, hammers were banging in nails, and the lights were going on and off. The engineer was testing the sound. Clem had to admit that it was a teeny bit less organized than the big Broadway shows. Those were so polished, there would never be any of this kind of scrambling. Although the scrambling did make it pretty exciting. There was a sense of urgency that she kind of liked.

Clem was wearing a *lot* of makeup. Under the lights, it felt kind of like her face was melting. While Abu climbed a ladder to adjust a hanging moon, she went backstage. She sat down at one of the empty makeup mirrors and inspected her face. The actors didn't seem to notice her. Their chatter rose and fell around her. By the light of the mirrors, her makeup looked really bad, like a *kid* had done it. "Embarrassing," she said, and stuck out her tongue at herself, even though she *was* a kid.

She'd followed a YouTube tutorial and she'd thought she looked really pretty when she first finished it. But looking pretty was such a mismatch with how she felt, so she'd added more and more and more black eyeliner until her face matched her insides, and then she'd just looked messy, like she'd colored outside the lines by mistake. She'd put the eyeliner in her pocket, just in case some smudged off. She took it out now and looked at it.

The eyeliner had come from One Buck Chuck. The rule was that they could take things from the store, they just had to write it in the book. She'd never really wanted anything before, but last week the eyeliner called her name.

Before Abu picked them up for *Dogs*, she could *see* her mom pretending not to notice what she had done to her face.

She could also see that Jorge and her dad genuinely *didn't* notice. It made her want to add more and more and more black until maybe she was completely obscured by eyeliner, like a sketch of herself that had been angrily scribbled out.

"Notice me!" she wanted to scream, at the same time as she wanted to shout, "Leave me alone!"

Abu had raised his eyebrows when he had seen her and said, "You've got your stage makeup on!" and she had finally felt *seen*, just for a second.

She uncapped the eyeliner and drew a tear on her cheek. It was really small. From a distance, it probably would just look like a freckle. She could pretty much guarantee that no one would see it for what it really was.

Clem walked out onto the stage. Her shoes squeaked a little on the wood, making her think of gym floors and Mr. Banks and his weird smells and barked orders. There was one other woman on the set adjusting some cables, but otherwise, it was the quietest place in the whole theater. Everyone else obviously had somewhere to be, some important something must have been happening elsewhere. The stage seemed to be holding itself as still as the unrippled surface of a pool, waiting for a diver to break through.

Clem took a deep breath and sat down at center stage, criss-cross applesauce. She made her spine as straight as she could and then she closed her eyes against all the colors and too-bright lights. The stage was as smooth as the tight skin of a drum, just like the stage at *TMTFIA*. She leaned forward until her forehead touched it and she bonked it gently.

She *remembered.*

She remembered how solid the *TMTFIA* stage was, how it didn't give even a little. She remembered how it felt like her bones crumpled under her skin, like the metal body of a car collapsing against a brick wall.

"Member," she said and frowned. She hadn't remembered to tell kit about that: Member. *Re*member. *De*member.

Oh, there was so much she wanted to *demember*, like how that landing was a sound that was a feeling that was a sound, how hitting the stage had felt like it was coming from the *inside* of her, not the outside. How it had felt like her lungs were overblown balloons that had burst.

Why had she patted that dog?

She should have *run* when it came toward her. She

should have let Jorge push it away. She knew better than to *touch* it.

She was so *stupid*.

"There's a kid on the stage!" someone called out from the darkness of the orchestra pit, and Clem felt insulted. Then Abu yelled back from somewhere behind Clem, "It's okay, she's mine!"

Clem knew she should get up and go help Jorge with the food, but she didn't. She pressed her hands flat against the stage. It must have looked like she was doing some form of praying, leaning forward like that, palms outstretched. *Maybe I* should *pray,* she thought.

Please, she tried.

But she wasn't sure what else to say. She didn't really know how to pray.

Please.

She held her breath. She could feel her heartbeat getting louder and louder and louder until it was drumming in her ears.

She felt like she was floating.

Or maybe like she should be able to stretch out her wings and fly.

She took a deep breath in and exhaled. Then she sat up. A bank of spotlights lit up, startling her for a second. It flashed through a series of blinding colors, and then shut off again.

A man came out from the wings and handed her a microphone. "If you're going to sit out here, you can help us test the sound, please. Something isn't connecting right with those back speakers. Opening night! Wouldn't you know it?"

"Yeah, okay. Fine," she said, trying to sound like she didn't care. She imagined how she looked to him with her makeup and her stomping boots, sitting there.

He grinned.

"You a theater kid?" He kept smiling at her, like she wasn't a terrifying black hole of a person who caused bad things to happen. "You've got the look down pat."

"Thanks," she said.

Clem stood up. The microphone felt heavy. She put it in one hand and then back into the other. She squinted at the empty seats in the audience. She imagined kit sitting there. "Be a turtle!" she'd be saying.

"Too turtle-y," she told kit, in her head.

"Be a non-turtle-y turtle!" kit would have said.

So predictable, she thought at the same time as she thought, *I miss kit.*

She didn't deserve kit. She was too mean. "Naked

mole rat," she whispered. Even saying it made her stomach hurt.

There was a rush of static from the speaker. Clem straightened up and pushed her hair behind her ears.

"What are you doing?" Jorge wandered over. "Why are you holding that?"

"Shhh," said Clem, more bravely than she felt and more loudly than she meant to. "Go away. I'm testing."

Jorge raised his eyebrows. "Okaaaay," he said. "But we have to go pick up the food." He waved the list at her. She saw the words "NO DRESSING" written in all-caps.

"I'm busy. This is, like, important." She flicked the microphone on and feedback screeched out of every corner of the place.

Jorge covered his ears. "Ouch, hey." His voice echoed around the stage.

"Not yet! Not yet!" the man yelled. "Turn it off, please!"

She turned it off. The spotlights flicked on for a second, then went to black light, which made Jorge's white shirt glow, then went off, too. Then the center lights pointed toward her and shone so brightly, she couldn't see anything at all.

The empty chairs disappeared.

Imaginary kit disappeared.

Jorge disappeared.

Clem was totally alone. She stretched out her arms.

"I'm going, then, I guess," Jorge said. "By myself. Or maybe I'll see if Abu can help me. It's a lot of stuff to carry."

Clem didn't answer. Her nose was itchy.

"Okay," a disembodied voice boomed. "Try saying *testing testing testing.*"

Clem turned the microphone back on. "*Testing testing testing,*" she repeated. Her voice was huge. It bounced around the empty space like thunder.

"Hang on," said the voice.

Three people dressed as dogs stepped out of the wings. They were wearing bodysuits that were black and brown and white, painted to look like fur, but not fluffy. Their makeup was super-detailed, with whiskers and glowing eyes, making their faces creepily and wonderfully doglike. They were very involved in an elaborate fist-bump routine, standing in a semicircle, eyes closed.

It looked like a ritual.

So much of being onstage was tied to luck and superstition. She knew that. She'd been practically *raised* in the theater.

"Again please," said the voice.

"*Testing testing testing,*" Clem said. And then she added, "*Woof, woof, woof.*" because she couldn't help it, because it was a show about dogs, after all. "Woof" was obviously dog for "testing." She half-smiled.

There was a buzz and crackle from the speaker, and then someone shouted, "DARN IT!"

"Hang on, kid," the voice said. "Off again."

"Hanging," she said, turning the microphone off. She leaned her head back and felt the lights on her face. They were warm, like the sun.

I belong here, she thought. Then she blushed. What if she'd said it out loud, by mistake? She snuck a glance at the dogs, but they showed no sign of having heard her. She exhaled.

Jim Jones, the leader of Jonestown, had loved the stage, too. She could tell by the way he had puffed up and looked larger than life once he was in front of a microphone. She watched a clip on YouTube of one of his famous speeches. It was a good, powerful speech but at the same time, she could totally tell he was bananas. Why hadn't her grandfather been able to see that there was something wrong with Jim Jones?

"You want me to be a father figure, I'll be your father figure," Jim Jones had bellowed into the microphone. "You want me to be your God? I. Will. Be. Your. God!"

The audience had gone wild, singing "hallelujah" and clapping, and, watching, Clem had felt a tug of that same *something* that was making them whoop.

It was a good feeling. She wasn't sure what she believed in, but she knew she believed in that feeling, the feeling of being part of a group of people who were all on the same page.

"I get it," she whispered, and for a second, she truly did, but it was a slippery feeling and then it was gone again. If Beau had known it was just a *feeling*, a feeling he could have got from, say, watching *Hamilton* or listening to a huge choir, then maybe he could have joined the theater instead of a doomed suicide cult.

"Hey, sorry," said the voice. "Can we try again?"

Clem dropped the microphone with a clatter and then bent and picked it up. "Yes?" But the microphone was off. "Sorry!"

"Turn it on and say something, please," the voice requested.

She turned it on. "Something," she repeated, her voice cracking. She cleared her throat and tried again. "SOMETHING."

"A little more, please. I mean, more words, not more volume."

Clem couldn't think of anything. She froze.

"Whenever you're ready."

"If you want me to be your father, I'll be your father. IF YOU WANT ME TO BE YOUR GOD, I WILL BE YOUR GOD!" She shouted the last part. There was a silence where her words seemed to echo around the theater, then another rush of static from the speaker.

"Okay," the voice went on, as though she hadn't just yelled something incredibly weird. "Can you sing? Do you know a song?"

"Yes." Clem thought about all the songs that she knew. What songs did she actually know the words to?

Kit had a portable orange record player that she had found for free on the sidewalk. She had that kind of luck, stumbling on perfect stuff like that, out of the blue. The record player didn't just play records, it was actually a really old-fashioned karaoke machine, with a microphone and everything. They only had one record to play on it, and that was kit's mom's record and they could only play it when kit's mom wasn't home because she said listening to it made her want to crawl out of her own skin.

After listening to it a million times, Clem had for sure learned the one main song. The song was called "Girls With Wings."

"I can sing something, I guess." She sounded more sure than she felt.

"Now's good," said the man, so Clem opened her mouth and started to sing.

At first her voice came out rough and wispy. Her legs started shaking, which was strange, and the shaking was coming through in the song. She pulled more air into her lungs and pushed out the words harder, from deeper inside her, until the strength and volume of her voice drowned out the quiver.

As her voice got louder, she understood that she could do it, that she could *sing*. Really sing.

She felt like a giant. She felt enormous.

She sang louder still.

She was glad Jorge wasn't there, because without him there, *seeing* her, she could be anyone. She could be someone who sang, someone who felt at home onstage, singing like she'd been born to do it, like she'd been made specifically to sing this song.

She felt *free*.

It felt *right*.

It was the *rightest* feeling she had ever had.

She felt one hundred percent happy.

When it was over, the three dogs who weren't really dogs stared at her, and then they slowly started to clap.

"Oh my good golly, girl," one of them called out. "You have some *pipes*."

"Chills! You gave me chills!" said another.

Clem smiled. "Um, thanks." She made a gesture that was sort of like a cross between a bow and a curtsy and the person did it back.

She felt like she could do anything in that moment, literally anything in the world.

She smiled.

It was the first true, big, honest, open smile she'd smiled in months. It made her face ache.

I can't wait to tell kit about this, she thought.

Then: *I* can't *tell kit about this.*

"Wow." Jorge walked toward her with a huge bag of food. The bag was almost as big as he was. "That was totally *amazing.*"

"Oh, what*ever.*" Clem put down the microphone and stomped off the stage, even though that wasn't anything like what she'd wanted to say at all.

"You could help with the bag!" Jorge yelled after her, but she didn't turn around, just kept walking until she couldn't hear him anymore.

kit

WHEN KIT ARRIVED AT THE SHELTER, SHE HAD A VERY STRANGE feeling inside her. It wasn't a *bad* feeling. Kind of the opposite. It was going to feel *good* to tell someone what happened. The idea of sharing it, even with Chandra, gave kit a powerful feeling, a feeling that made her think of supernovas, something impossibly bright and quiet.

But kit didn't tell Chandra about Jackson's letter or about Clem or about *the thing that happened* because before she was even all the way through the front door, Chandra was already talking.

Yelling, really.

"They're going to do it, kit," she yelled, throwing her phone down so hard that kit was surprised it didn't break. "Those morons. They *suck*. They are terrible people. They're doing it and there's nothing we can do about it and life is not fair, that's the truth."

She pounded her fist on the counter. It made a hammer-nail sound because of all her rings, which were big, lumpy skulls.

"They." *Bang.*

"Are." *Bang.*

"Monsters." *Bang.*

A second later, Max—a giant black dog with a sad brown face—was standing next to her, his front paws on the counter, like he worked there. Kit imagined a talking bubble above his head saying, "Can I help you?" Dogs weren't supposed to be in the reception area in case customers were allergic or afraid. Kit didn't know why someone allergic to or afraid of dogs would be at an animal shelter in the first place but obviously she wasn't in any position to question the management. She didn't even know exactly who the management were. The only person she ever saw at the shelter was Chandra, and sometimes the vet, who they called Dr. Big Smile, because he was always grinning too widely.

"Who?" kit said. "What? Hi Max, Max, Max." If her own name was all lower-case because she was too small for capital letters, then Max, who was huge even for a rottweiler, should have been all-caps. "MAX," she said. She couldn't see his stubby tail, but she could tell that it was wagging. "MAXIMUM MAX."

She had seen a whole photo series online: dogs' faces before and after you asked them if they were a good dog. It was the best thing that had ever been on the internet, in her opinion. "Who's a good boy?" she said.

Max smiled.

"*You're* the good boy," said kit. "You are."

Chandra glared at kit. "*Them.* And *him,*" she nodded at Max. She put her hands over his ears. "They're putting him down," she hissed.

"Putting him down" meant killing him. Everyone knew that. But still, for a second, kit tried hearing it a different way. She *wanted* it to mean something else. "Putting him down" could mean just that they insulted him. Maybe.

"Why are you just staring?" said Chandra. "Say something."

Kit grimaced.

"Are you *smiling*? There is literally no way you can be smiling right now. I'm so mad, I feel like I could spit nails," Chandra said. "Or something bigger than nails. What's bigger than a nail?"

"I'm not smiling. A rail tie?"

"I don't even know what that is."

"Oh." Kit didn't know how she knew what they were, but she did. "They're big spikes used to nail down train tracks."

"Well then, yes, I could spit a rail tie. Don't you get it? They are going to *murder* Max."

"I get it." Kit put her hand on Max's back and felt her knees go soft. She slumped against the counter. "We have to stop them," she whispered.

"No *kidding,*" Chandra said. "That's what I've been saying. We have to adopt him out ASAP. Like, today."

Kit scratched Max's *spot,* which was behind his left ear. When you scratched him there, his leg thumped.

"Why are we called a shelter if we just *kill* the dogs? The world is horrible. Even do-gooder places like this are basically just tools of the evil oppressors."

"The evil oppressors," kit echoed. She liked how that sounded Star Wars-ish. She imagined them all jumping into some kind of triangular spaceship and jetting off into space, but Star Wars also made her think of Jackson, which made her feel annoyed. Again. "That sucks."

"*Everything* sucks," said Chandra.

"I read about this guy once—a window washer – he fell off a forty-seven-story building and he didn't die."

"What? *When*?"

"I don't know, a long time ago. Not, like, *yesterday.* I found it when I was looking up stuff after Clem's accident. I wanted to see what people could survive."

"Well, I don't know what that has to do with Max," Chandra said, scathingly.

The world sometimes catches you gently in its hand, was what kit wanted to say, but couldn't because that wasn't how normal kids talked.

But that's what she'd *meant.*

But then she wondered if it was even true because sometimes the world was looking away when you fell, and BAM.

"The sky is falling, the sky is falling," kit said.

"True fact," said Chandra. "The sky *is* always falling. And there is nothing we can do to get out of the way." She slapped the counter to punctuate her metaphor. She was angry about everything, like Clem. Maybe *angry* was the phase everyone went through and Clem was early to it and Chandra was late. Kit tried to imagine herself being that way, but she couldn't. Not really.

Max got down, his claws scraping smoothly along the surface of the counter. He was *alive.* That was the important thing. He wasn't dead *yet.* It was hard to imagine that he *could* be. He put his giant head against kit's leg, like he understood she needed help staying up.

"I'm going to put pics of him on Pictasnap," said Chandra. "Maybe he'll go viral. People are a sucker for a sad story. I'm going to say that he saved a baby from a fire. More than one baby. A *bunch* of babies. And kittens. Every idiot in the world loves kittens."

"Did he save any kittens? Or babies?"

"Duh, no. Obviously not. But who knows what his story was before he came here? It's not impossible that he saved a cat. Or a kid."

Kit thought about this. "It just seems like a lot. People might Google it and then find out right away that you made it up. Maybe say that he stopped a man from breaking into someone's apartment and robbing it." She thought about this. "A man wearing a Batman mask!"

"A *Batman mask*? That's oddly specific."

"It's the kind of detail that makes it seem real." Kit wondered if the Batman guy had stolen a TV yet and if he'd scared anyone to death in the process.

"Fine," said Chandra. "A Batman mask. Whatever. Move over so I can take a good pic of him."

Kit moved. She took off her glasses and polished them on her T-shirt and watched Max posing blurrily.

Without her glasses on, everything in the room looked as soft and harmless as cotton balls. She took Jackson's stupid purple-inked note out of her pocket. When she was little, she would only do her schoolwork with purple pen because she thought the black ink was too sharp at the edges. Jackson is the only one she told. That used to be how it was, she would tell him all her weird stuff and he would make her feel less weird about it. *Sharp black* versus *soft purple* was their inside joke for ages and ages.

But now she hated him for thinking their in-joke was still something they shared. It wasn't. He lost all his rights to their in-jokes when he did what he did.

She hesitated, still holding on to the musty folded paper, but then Chandra started talking again.

"I wish we could make him look less *snarly*. He looks like Cujo. That was a dog in a horror movie which I'm sure you haven't seen, kiddo. At least, I hope not. It was cheesy but also super scary." She contemplated Max. "I'm going to take a profile so his messed up lip doesn't wreck his chances." She scratched him behind the ear and then kissed his head. "We'll save you, buddy."

Kit swallowed. She didn't want to cry.

"You're not supposed to be behind the counter," Chandra said, sitting back down.

"I know. Unofficial, remember?" Kit planned to officially volunteer as soon as she turned thirteen. That would be in five months and eighteen days. It seemed like both a long time and not a long enough time to stay twelve, to be a *kid*.

"Well, stay low if anyone comes in." Chandra sighed. She took a pen out of the mug on the counter and poked it through her ear stretcher, balancing it there.

"I could try asking Mom if we could take him."

Even as kit said it, she knew it was impossible but it felt important to say it.

Chandra snorted. "Is she still afraid to go to a movie?"

"We watch movies at home."

"Seriously, when was the last time she went out?"

Kit frowned. "She went down to get Diet Coke yesterday from the bodega."

"But that building is attached to your building! It's not even technically leaving the building! Your mom is going to get scurvy or whichever thing you get when you don't get any sun."

"Rickets," said kit. She'd looked it up. "Max would be good for her. She'd have to take him for walks, right? And he could protect her from . . . " She stopped herself. She *almost* said "men wearing Batman masks."

"Forget it," Chandra said. "She wouldn't be able to walk him and then he'd get fat."

"I could walk him."

"She wouldn't say yes. She's like my stepmom, except different. But both of them are not pet people." She paused, then added, "Freaks."

"Hey," said kit. "My mom isn't a freak. She's just . . ." She searched for the word. "Delicate." She pictured the *Argentinosaurus* constellation of fears, marching slowly down the street, bowling pedestrians and cars out of its way. There was nothing delicate about titanosaurs.

There was nothing delicate about Max either, which is why he'd be a good match for everything her mom was afraid of.

The sun was pooling in on the waiting room floor and making a rainbow on the linoleum. Max lay his giant head on kit's leg and groaned, as if this photo session was more than he could take on top of his impending death. Kit could feel his hot breath through her jeans.

"Life is brutal to the ugly," Chandra went on, uploading the photo on her phone. "I hope one day, the uglies take over the world. I'm including you and me in that. You know what I mean."

Kit did know what Chandra meant and also she was

the only person in the world who would say right to kit's face "You're ugly!" and somehow make it sound like that was preferable to being gorgeous. Chandra wasn't ugly at all. She was beautiful but she didn't think she was because she had a big birthmark that covered exactly half her face. She said it looked like clown makeup but she was wrong. Her iridescent pale blue hair was what people noticed first. Kit didn't love hair, in general, but she loved Chandra's.

"So," she said, but Chandra wasn't listening. She was pacing around the waiting room. Kit turned her "so" into a cough. Chandra was pretty much for sure the wrong person to share things with, she already knew that. Everything kit told her would just make her angrier and probably wouldn't help. She tucked the letter back in her pocket.

Chandra sat down right in the rainbow reflection in one smooth motion, like a ballerina. The rainbow shone on her jeans, making them look iridescent. Max went over and nudged her with his nose. "He's saving me! Good boy," she said. "There, we have evidence that he's a saver. I'm posting this."

"Good," said kit.

"This is a life lesson, kit. A good person doesn't always come in and save the day. Most days suck and most people are bad and the good people are, like, busy stopping other people from jumping off bridges and they don't have the time or energy to adopt black rotty mixes."

"I know that. I get it. I *hear* you." She paused. "How many good people are saving people from jumping off bridges right now?"

"I don't know! Lots. None. Okay, fine: one. Before you came in, I was listening to a podcast about a guy in China who walks around every day pulling jumpers off railings."

"In China, not here?"

"Yeah, China. That's what I said." Chandra nudged kit with her boot, which was as close as she came to affection. Max had fallen asleep, as though the conversation had just gone ahead and bored him halfway to the death that was inevitable. He farted, which woke him up. He startled and sniffed himself suspiciously. "Maybe we should just let him go out the door to find his own way in this cruel world. Wow, that stinks, Max."

Chandra reached into her backpack and took out a sandwich. She never ate anything normal and this sandwich was another one of her weird concoctions: banana and mayo on white bread. Kit tried the sandwich once. Eating it was exactly like what it would probably be like to eat a mouthful of the banana-scented hair paste that her mom used at the salon.

Chandra sniffed the sandwich and then unwrapped it and gave half to Max. He ate it in a single gulp, wriggling with joy.

"We could just let him go in the park," Chandra said. Her shirt, which had a picture on it of a woman raising her fist, was freckled with crumbs. "Then he could be free, like animals were meant to be. There was a *cow* running through there the other day. An actual cow! Did you see it? I was definitely Team Cow."

Kit shook her head.

"People can't stand to see stuff out of context," Chandra went on. "They were going crazy. The cow didn't care. To the cow, it was just a field. But people were like, 'Doesn't that cow know that this is Brooklyn?' But Max wouldn't be out of context."

Kit thought about all the people running and riding bikes through the park.

She thought about the way their feet flew.

She thought about the way the bike wheels glinted in the sun.

She had walked Max enough times to know that he could *not* see someone running or riding a bike without chasing them.

"Max chases people at the park. He can't help it."

"Then it's his own fault that no one has adopted him, I guess." Chandra scowled and crumpled up her lunch bag. "He's his own worst enemy."

"He doesn't mean to be." Kit wrapped her arms around him. His chest was wider than hers, so her arms barely reached all the way around him. He closed one eye as though he was winking at her and sighed tolerantly.

"He's winking."

"Dogs don't like being hugged."

"Yeah," kit said, letting go, even though Max was leaning into the hug. "You're right."

Agreeing with Chandra was the best way to get along with Chandra. "Hey, can I ask you something?" Kit took the letter out of her pocket again. Chandra looked at her, but then her attention jumped to someone who was about to come in the door. "Oh, brother. *This* should be good. Get down and hang on to Max, kit. Last thing we need is for him to knock this one over."

Kit ducked behind the counter with Max as the door made its usual sad battery-dying buzz sound. Chandra didn't get up off the stool.

Max didn't budge, but kit wove her hand under his collar, just in case. Not that she could have held him back. He weighed at least a hundred pounds and she was sixty-two pounds, last time she checked. She put Jackson's stupid purple-penned note in the garbage. Her dad was the Night Sky and she didn't care that he *technically* wasn't. Maybe he was really this man named John Alexander Findley who had died two years ago on April 14, a name and date that she didn't even want to know in the first place and now couldn't forget. Then she took the note out of the garbage and put it back into her pocket.

"Yes, yes," she heard a woman's voice saying. "I know. I heard you."

"We don't have all day here, ma'am, awfully busy, don't you know," Chandra cooed in an obviously fake British accent. The lady must have been oblivious to Chandra's simmering anger (which kit knew often took the form of bad accents and sarcasm) because she was still talking on the phone. Kit couldn't see her from where she was sitting, but she could hear her. She sounded like a *mom*. Not *her* mom, but someone's mom.

"I *told* you so," the woman said. "I said that already. We can discuss this after you get your homework done. Please go do it."

"Hallo," Chandra interrupted. "Hallo. Oh, I see you're just having a chat on the telephone. I'll just wait, shall I? Jolly good."

Kit ducked her head down so that her laugh didn't escape. She focused on Chandra's legs, which were as bristly as a scrubbing brush. She refused to shave them to please the patriarchy. When Chandra had heard who kit's mom used to be, she had gasped out loud. "She's my idol! That song. Wow."

"What is she doing?" Chandra muttered to kit. "Come on already. Hang up the phone! Then let's play What's in the Box?"

"I'm here now, I said. I've got to go. I'm hanging up, they're waiting for me," the woman's voice said. "I'm hanging up *right now*. I love you. Wait there. I'll be back in a minute."

Then, "Sorry to keep you waiting. I'm just, I'm a bit, I'm, you know, flustered, I suppose. Animals make me . . . I don't like . . . "

"Quite all right," said British Chandra. "What have you got there then, guv'nor?"

Kit snort-laughed.

There was the sound of high heels clicking across the tile entrance and approaching the counter.

Click-click-click.

Kit wondered if the shoes had red soles, if they cost as much as a month's rent, if they were as uncomfortable as she imagined. She wondered if the lady's face winced every time she took a step. She wanted to pop her head up to look, but then it would seem weird that she'd hidden in the first place.

When kit's mom used to wear the red-soled shoes, which was only when she went somewhere fancy—so not lately at all, obviously—she looked like she was floating in them, just a tiny fraction of an inch above the ground. But when kit tried, she couldn't even take two steps in them. They hurt every bone in her feet and ankles and even her legs. They were like torture devices.

Now red-soled shoes made her think of her mom's photo above the fireplace, where she was smiling and there was something wide open about her happiness. Thinking about it made kit want to cry because mostly when her mom smiled now, it never illuminated her whole face like that. Her smiles were small and taut, her mouth curling up only slightly at the corners.

Kit heard the gentle thud of something landing on the counter. "What *is* it?" Chandra repeated, impatiently.

The woman took a deep breath. Kit could hear her whistle-y inhale. "My son found this poor thing in the park. Half-dead, I think. Or in shock. In the sandbox. Some kids had buried it." Her voice was shaking.

Jackson, kit thought, which she knew was *bananas* but she also knew she was right. She knew that woman's voice. That was Jackson's mom. And Jackson would love rescuing some weird animal, just so that people would think he was a hero. He liked to think of himself as one, anyway. Old Jackson would never hurt an animal, but with New Jackson, who knew?

"People can be so awful," Jackson's mom said, and kit agreed silently.

"That's the truth," Chandra said, in her normal voice.

"I promised my son that I'd take it to the shelter. I guess you'll probably kill it or just let it die or even feed it to the snakes, but don't tell me that because I don't want to lie to him. Please. I really don't. I can't. I won't ever lie. He deserves better than that. He's been through a lot, with my husband, well, he . . . left. Last year. You think you know someone." She was talking really fast. She sounded as though she was going to cry.

Max tensed up. He didn't like it when people were upset. He growled, low and deep.

"Max," kit whispered. "Good boy. It's okay."

"Sad story," Chandra interrupted. Kit could practically *hear* her rolling her eyes. "But we don't *do* rodents, lady."

Rodents.

The word "rodent" made kit's throat start to close up. Chandra stepped back, nearly standing on kit's hand, and kit heard the door opening and closing, moaning sadly.

"Just take it," the lady said, firmly. "Please. Thank you."

"Mom, can we get a dog while we're here?" another voice said.

Jackson. Kit's heart stopped cold in her chest and then started again with a stutter-y beat.

"Please. Let's just look at them," Jackson said.

Max twisted out of kit's grip and jumped up on the counter, wagging his stubby tail.

"Oh my *gosh*," said Jackson. "Hey, buddy, where did you come from? Look Mom, this dog likes me. He wants to come with us, don't you, dude?"

"NO," kit shouted, without even thinking about what she was doing. "No."

Chandra kicked kit and glared at her. "You are welcome to fill out an application. Max is a lovely, good dog. He'd make someone a great pet." She picked up an application form.

Kit clenched her fists. She wanted Max to be saved. But by *Jackson*?

"Who is behind the counter? Who said no?"

"*No,* honey," said Jackson's mom. "I don't know who said it, but I'm saying it. We're leaving. We'll talk about a dog. Maybe. We'll ask your dad. But you know how he feels about dogs. You know how *I* feel about dogs."

"He's *not* my dad. He's my *step*dad. And you said I could get another dog after Dad gave Archibald to the farmer."

"Honey, Archie is dead. I'm not going to pretend that he's living on a farm, I'm sorry. That's a lie."

There was a long silence. Then, "*Jeez,* Mom. That's harsh. There was probably a better way to tell me that."

Kit swallowed. She blinked. Did she hear that right? *Poor Jackson,* she thought.

Jackson's mom's phone started ringing. "Jackson, we have to . . . I need to get this call."

"But Mom, that dog *chose* me, look at him! He even looks like Archie!"

"Archie was a *beagle,*" Jackson's mom said. "Are you trying to be funny?"

"It's not how he looks, exactly, it's his *expression.*"

"Goodbye," said Chandra. "Thank you for the . . . " She tapped the box. "Thing. Did I mention we don't do rodents?"

"You've got, like, an obligation to save it, right? Like

if someone leaves their baby in a box at the fire hall?" Jackson asked.

"Oh yeah, kid, it's just like that." Chandra snort-laughed. "Same thing."

"I hope you're not lying to me."

"Definitely not, my man," said Chandra. "Saving is our game."

"JACKSON!"

"I'm COMING!"

Kit heard the clicking of the heels and the squeak of Jackson's sneakers and the sad door sound and then there was silence, except for the sound of Max panting slightly, her own breathing, and the skittering sound of the animal in the box.

"I'm not even going to *ask*," said Chandra. "But if they apply for Max, they might save his life, you know."

"I know," said kit.

"So? What's your problem with that kid?"

Kit thought about how to answer. "He used to be my best friend," was what almost came out, but she stopped it. "He's in my class," is what she said instead, which wasn't enough, but it would have to do.

Chandra swore out loud, a word kit's mom would have killed her for saying. Then she said, "Get up, kit. You've got to see this. This is the ugliest, weirdest thing that I've ever seen. This thing makes Max look like he should be competing in beauty pageants."

"What is it?" Kit suddenly had a sinking, strange, shivery feeling. She hopped up and down—which was awkward in skates—because her legs were asleep, but that wasn't really the problem.

Kit peered over the edge of the box, which was a new-looking Adidas shoe box with a price tag on the end that said $399.99.

That is a crazy amount of money to spend on shoes, she thought.

Chandra tipped the box toward kit. Inside, there was a very wrinkled up . . . *something.*

It was *definitely* a rodent.

A very specific type of rodent.

It was a *naked mole rat.*

Just like kit had known it would be, without realizing that she'd known, that it was what it *had* to be. It was like an audible *click* that she felt in her mind when what she saw caught up to what she'd guessed.

"Oh boy," she said.

kit

KIT STARTED TO COUGH.

"Are you choking?"

Kit shook her head, no, but she was. She coughed and gasped.

"Get a drink of water or something! Don't die on my watch."

Kit couldn't take her eyes off the naked mole rat. When she finally caught her breath, she tried to say "Naked mole rat!" but it came out all scratchy and wrong.

"Holy cow," said Chandra, poking it with a pen.

Kit wanted to cover it up with something: a tiny hat, scarf, and coat. *Definitely* pants. "Don't," she said, and took the pen out of Chandra's hand.

The feeling of *the thing that happened* surged through her, but this time with more force, like lightning coming from the ground up through her skates and out her skull.

"I'm . . . "

"What are you doing? This thing is *fantastically* hideous. I think I love it." Chandra picked up the box and the animal inside started scrabbling around, like it was trying to get a grip on the cardboard.

"Do you ever think—" kit was suddenly feeling strangely out of breath, like she'd been running and the feelings in her heart and brain were getting worse—"That everything is kind of connected?"

"I guess. I mean, we're all definitely part of one big food chain. You don't even want to *know* where humans are on that."

"The . . . top?"

Chandra looked at kit, then she laughed. "You're right, I guess."

She reached into the shoebox and lifted out the animal. It was motionless in her hand, as if panic had depleted it of every last bit of its energy. Or maybe it was dead. "Who is the ugliest baby?" Chandra crooned. "Hey kit, this thing could be our mascot."

"It's a naked mole rat," kit said, louder. She was *really* dizzy.

"You're right!" said Chandra. "It *is* a naked mole rat. That's so cool, I can't even. I've never seen one for real."

"I saw them at the Bronx Zoo." Seeing the animals for the first time was when kit realized that it was a pretty insulting thing for her mom to say when she called kit "my little naked mole rat." She'd never liked it, but seeing one for real drove it home. Pictures couldn't capture their true weirdness. She must have made a face because the guide had said, "Don't be grossed out! These little dudes are superheroes!"

"They can go without air for eighteen minutes," kit said to Chandra now. Her whole body felt like it was asleep, pins and needles prickled everywhere. She shook her arms out. "They live in families, like bees. There's a queen. They never get cancer. They live for way longer than other animals because they don't get sick. They can run just as fast backward as they can run forward. They don't feel pain." She thought about the last part. "Which must be nice."

"All life is suffering," said Chandra.

"What?"

"It's Buddhist." Chandra lifted the animal higher and inspected it on all sides. "If these are super rare, maybe we can sell it for cash as an artisanal pet for hipsters."

Kit was definitely not feeling well. The room was spinning.

"On the other hand, the whole thing with hipsters is hair-related. Like beards and handlebar mustaches."

"Give it to me," kit said.

"No! You're not even an official volunteer!" Chandra put the naked mole rat on her shoulder.

"It *is* me," kit whispered, which she knew was true, even though it couldn't be.

"You can't *have* it. I'm sure your mom has naked-mole-rat-o-phobia. There's no way."

"I *can* have it. I am it." Kit's voice was so faint, she wondered if Chandra even heard her.

"We'll put it in a cage for now and figure it out in the morning." Chandra looked at the clock. "We're closing in ten minutes and I have a movie to go to the second we close. *And* it's the opening night and I won't let you and this rat make me miss it."

"It will die in the cage! They get cold. They can't regulate their body temperature." Kit tried to shout but her voice came out in a stretched groan, like the sad dead-battery sound the door made when it opened.

She was cold. *She* couldn't regulate her body temperature.

She needed to go. She had to get out of there. *It* needed to get out of there.

"You are like an encyclopedia of naked mole rat facts. That's pretty weird, kiddo."

Kit shivered violently.

"Your mom would kill you if I let you take it. And I'm, like, sorry your mom is a nutbar, but I'm not giving you this rat. If it's diseased and you get the disease, your mom will sue the shelter and then it will have to close down."

"She would n-n-never!"

"You don't know that! You should wash your hands, by the way."

"I didn't touch it!"

"I have to go. I'm locking up."

"NO," kit whisper-shouted with all her strength. "It will die!"

Faster than she had ever done anything, kit reached over and grabbed the naked mole rat right out of Chandra's hand. It felt like someone else was doing it.

Someone who was kit but also who was not kit.

Someone a lot braver and bigger than kit.

Someone who was not even a little bit scared of Chandra, with her blue hair and Doc Martens and giant stretchers in her ears and her black lipstick.

"What are you doing? You don't even work here!"

"Unofficial!" kit managed to say.

"Give it back!"

The naked mole rat was trying to escape. It was rubbery and cold and strange in kit's hand, as though its skin was made from a too-big latex glove. It squirmed and scratched. Kit could feel its heart tapping fast against her palm and her own heart speeding up to match it.

She could also hear Chandra yelling at her, but she couldn't make out what she was saying.

She thought about the window washer who fell, how it must have felt for him, wiping his squeegee against the glass one second and in the next second seeing the window moving away from his hand and thinking, "Is the *building* falling?" before he realized that the thing that was falling was him.

She thought about Clem falling, how maybe she thought, "Is the *stage* moving?"

It's exactly how kit felt, right then, like she was standing still and everything fell away from her:

Chandra. The room of cages. Max, whining and whimpering. The fluorescent lights. The tile floor. The smell of ammonia.

The naked mole rat opened its mouth wide. Kit could blurrily see its two huge front teeth. It looked like the naked mole rat smiled at her.

Then it casually stretched, and sank its yellow teeth directly into the soft web of skin between her thumb and her fingers.

Kit screamed.

She tried to drop it, but it was attached. She waved her hand up and down frantically.

"KIT!" Chandra yelled. "Put it down! Throw it in the cage!"

"Help!" Kit didn't want to hurt it, but it was sure hurting her.

Then a bunch of things happened at the same time:

Chandra grabbed kit's hand and banged it hard against the table, so hard that kit could feel it, mysteriously, in her own head.

"Ouch!"

It was very confusing.

It happened in slow motion.

Chandra touched her birthmark. "You look strange. Oh man, I'm going to *faint*," she said. And she did, sliding in slow motion onto the floor.

"CHANDRA!" kit tried to yell, but her voice was gone for real now.

Her ears were ringing.

Her eyes felt stuck half-closed.

Everything was so, so, so blurry.

Time did a hiccup.

Kit did a hiccup.

She turned inside out and then right side in again, or at least, that was how it felt.

Her body heaved.

Everything spun.

Everything stank.

Then she was on the floor, too.

She was *really* dizzy.

She tried to blink, but her eyelids didn't want to work. She could see light and a shape that she knew was Chandra. The shape wasn't moving. "Wake up," kit tried to say. But nothing came out.

Chandra seemed *really* big.

Then bigger.

Then *huge*.

Like an actual mountain.

Kit's blood felt like mud trying to swish through her spongy heart.

The room was so *dark* and loud.

Then she heard something that wasn't coming from *inside* her gloppy, sticky brain, a clattering and a scratching and a thumping, all at once. It got closer and closer and smelled worse and worse and she knew that smell, because duh.

That smell was dog drool.

Only it wasn't regular Max, it was *giant* Max.

And even though kit's eyes were all messed up without her glasses on, she could see teeth, and they looked really, *really* huge.

This was the third time it happened, so kit *knew* what was happening, knew that even though this *felt* different, it was also the same.

She was becoming the naked mole rat.

It was happening again.

The only difference was that now she knew for sure what she had become.

Kit did the only thing she could do: run.

She ran without thinking about where she was going. She ran right up the edge of the counter and over the top, past the giant shoe box, and up to the top of the computer screen.

Doing a quick scan of the room, she registered two shapes. The shape that wasn't moving was Chandra. And the shape that was moving was Max.

She didn't *think* because she couldn't, not really, she simply did what her heart was telling her to do, and she started to run again, down off the counter, to the door, up the glass, out through the mail slot, *running running running* along the sidewalk around dead leaves and garbage and feet and pigeons and dogs and other rats, *haired* rats.

She didn't even know anything could run so fast as she was running. She ran like she was flying and maybe she was.

Running like this felt like being part of the wind, part of the weather, part of everything in a way she never had been before.

It was better than flying.

Who needs wings? she thought.

She ran up the steps of the salon and then up the side of the building and up the fire escape and in through the kitchen window that she always left open a crack.

She ran to the bathroom, where the oils and herbs were lined up on a shelf.

She ran up the wall to the shelf, knocking them all into the bathtub. She ran through the slippery mess of Truth and Bravery and Courage and Love and Good Fortune. Then, smelling like roses and cloves and cinnamon and rosemary and thyme and tea tree oil and sandalwood and sage and who-even-knew-what, she ran into her room, burrowed deep into the blankets, and made herself slow down.

She didn't really mean to, but she closed her eyes and instead of falling asleep it was more like she just stopped, like *everything* stopped. And that was okay, too, because sometimes *everything* is a lot to take in and stopping is all that you can do, at least temporarily.

The next thing kit heard was her alarm clock beeping and her mom knocking on her door, saying, "Time to get up!" She stretched out her arms and they were just her regular arms. "I'm coming!" she called, and then the day started just like every other day, and she was kit again.

But she also was the naked mole rat.

And naked mole rats were superheroes, the man at the zoo had said so, and suddenly kit knew he was right. A thing didn't have to *look* powerful to *be* powerful. Neither did a person.

"Why don't you call me your little naked mole rat anymore?" kit asked her mom, as she hugged her goodbye.

Her mom kissed her head. "I guess when I really thought about it, it didn't sound like a compliment."

"It isn't," kit agreed. "But it also sort of *is*. Naked mole rats are cool."

Her mom smiled. "You know who is cool?"

"Who?"

"You are."

"Thanks, Mom."

"And you smell good." Kit's mom pressed her nose against kit's scalp. "What is that smell today?"

"Everything," kit said. "I smell like everything."

16 Clem

"I DON'T WANT TO DO THIS ANYMORE," SAID CLEM. IT WAS HARD for her to talk because she was balancing on her hands. Her face was turning purple. She couldn't blow enough air into her words so it came out more like, "Doughwhattodosmore." Her hands were clamped around Jorge's feet, which stank, which is part of the reason why it was hard to take a deep breath. He was standing on his hands, too. Her own feet were almost, but not quite, the same level as the living room light that was already hanging sideways from last time she accidentally kicked it. She bent her knees a little bit and then flipped off Jorge's feet onto the thick carpet with a muffled thud. She was sweating. When she landed, the pain shot through her left side like a bullet.

Jorge didn't answer. *He must be mad*, she thought.

So she didn't say the second thing she wanted to say, which was that, for the talent show, she didn't want to do an act with him at all.

She wanted to *sing*.

By herself.

It was a new thing for her to want and when she thought about it, the glass lump in her throat shivered. Having a *good* secret did that. It felt like the best thing that had happened to her since before the accident, but she also felt like maybe she shouldn't be happy, at least not anything more than fifty percent. She didn't know how to stop being fifty percent *dark*.

Clem bent at the waist. Her body knew what to do, even if she didn't *like* doing it. And even if it hurt.

"Huh?" said Jorge. He rolled into an easy somersault and lay flat.

"Huh *what*?" Clem stretched her arms behind her back until her bones made a satisfying crackling sound. Her head was itchy with sweat.

"Huh *what* did you say before? I didn't hear you." Jorge was scratching his head vigorously and energetically with both hands, like a dog going after a flea. "You said something."

"I can't remember what I said," Clem lied. Repeating it felt impossible.

She looked at the couch, which was squishy and covered in yellow velvet. It was so tempting to climb onto it and to curl up and sleep. It was piled high with cushions. No one ever really sat on it. They weren't exactly a couch family. They were an always-*moving* family. Her parents had a frenetic energy, all the time, like if they stopped moving, they would drop dead, like sharks.

"Did you know that sharks drown if they stop swimming?"

"That's not true," said Jorge. "They just basically faint."

"Oh."

"Don't try to sound deep."

"I'm not. Why are you being mean? You're the nice one, remember?" She hadn't been trying to sound like anything. She was already deep. Deep enough.

"I don't have to be nice all the time. I'm a *person*, you know. I can be in a bad mood."

She raised her eyebrows. "What's with you today? I thought you wanted to do this."

"I do."

"So, we're doing it, okay? Happy?"

He shrugged.

She opened her mouth to say, "I actually don't want to do it, Jorge." She thought maybe she'd say, "I'm sorry." But nothing came out.

She wondered what Beau would have said if she had gone to him and said, "I want to do something different from everyone else. I want to do something new."

She had a feeling he would say, "You do you, grand-girl!" Or "YOLO!"

He seemed like a YOLO kind of person.

What other kind of person would run off and join a cult? He believed in utopia! Probably also unicorns! It was no coincidence that the words were similar.

Clem walked over and lay down on the couch.

"What are you *doing*?"

"Lying on the couch," she said.

She'd sat on the couch when they first got it and her mom had burst out laughing. "Why are you *sitting*?" she'd said, as though sitting on a couch was the strangest thing in the world. What was it for if not sitting? Clem had felt embarrassed and lazy, even though she knew her mom didn't mean for it to sound that way.

Still, even after she got hurt, she made herself keep moving all the time. If she stopped moving, even when she was in the hospital, she'd hear her mom's voice saying, "Why are you *sitting*?"

"Do you ever think about just never doing this anymore?" Jorge asked, suddenly. "Do you ever want to just stop?"

"What do you mean?" Clem asked, even though she'd been thinking the exact same thing. She moved to the ground and did the splits. She used to be able to do them easily but now her hip sang with pain, like someone playing a bad note on a violin. "Give up all this?"

"We don't *have* to do it," Jorge said, quietly. "We can *not* do it."

"No, we *can't* not. It's what we do. Mom and Dad would be really disappointed."

"Mom and Dad don't do it anymore."

"They're just busy."

"Duh, no, they're old and it hurts now. It hurts you, too."

"Does not." She didn't know why she was lying. He was saying exactly what she wanted. She *wanted* to stop.

She lay back on the carpet and stared up at the light fixture. The glass was amber and the lightbulb glowed like a golden orb. It was really pretty. She'd never noticed how nice it was before.

"We can do something different for the talent show." Jorge cleared his throat. "You should sing."

"No," Clem said. She didn't know why she said that.

"You're a really good singer, Clem."

She shrugged. "I don't know how to sing. I've never had lessons or anything."

He sat down next to her. "Are you crazy? I heard you. You know how to sing."

"What would you do if I sang?"

"I could stuff myself through the top of a tennis racket."

"Like an octopus escaping from a fishing boat!" she said, mimicking their dad's voice.

"Escape artist!" he said, and laughed their dad's laugh. Then he stood up and bowed so deeply, his head touched the ground.

They both laughed.

"I don't think I could do it." She didn't look at him. Staring at the light was starting to make a sunspot in her vision. She blinked.

"Duh, of course you could." He sounded like it was no big deal. He didn't sound like he thought it was weird at all.

Clem felt something loosen in her chest. It felt like it was opening, like a lock or handcuffs. She nudged him. "Thanks."

He shrugged. "It's good if we do different stuff sometimes."

Later, up in her room, Clem got out her laptop and opened the school website. There was a talent show registration button, and she clicked it. "Clementine Garcia," she typed. "Singing." Then she clicked SUBMIT. Her heart felt light and strange, like a prop of something that's heavy in real life, but when you pick it up, you realize it's made of foam, that it's light as air.

She took a screenshot of her filled-out form. *Maybe I'll send the screenshot to kit,* she thought. She wanted kit to understand that *something* had changed, that she wasn't quite so mad or sad or whatever it was now, that maybe everything would be okay after all. Then she didn't do it. She wanted to, she just didn't.

kit

"CLEM," KIT SAID OUT LOUD. SHE WAS PRACTICING. "SO, HEY, the thing is that sometimes when I get super panicky, I turn into a naked mole rat. You were right about it, after all! So I forgive you! Even though you couldn't have known it was true! Ha ha!"

The "ha ha" felt forced and awkward, so she tried it again, without that part.

Then again.

And again.

The empty apartment bounced her words around. The plants seemed to be laughing at her, or maybe rolling their eyes.

"You're just going through a phase," she told them, then she made a face at herself in the mirror. She went downstairs to the salon to use the computer. It was Saturday, so she didn't have to go to school and spend all day trying to avoid Clem and Jorge again.

"You're up!" her mom said. She was sweeping the floor. The cut hair always made kit feel sad, like maybe it didn't understand how it came to be on the floor or where its owner went.

"I slept in," said kit. "I was tired."

Her mom kissed the top of kit's head, her hair swooping down and tickling kit's scalp like lemon-scented feathers. "Oh, good news!" She smiled at kit. "I didn't show you this yesterday!" She walked across to the front desk of the salon, her heels clicking, and came back. She was holding an envelope. Kit's heart dropped. Was it from Jackson? Did her mom know?

"What is it?"

"It turns out now that the song is getting played again, I'm getting royalties!" She opened the envelope and kit's eyes landed on the number. "It's being played a lot."

"Holy cow," kit said.

"I know!" Her mom did a spin, her dress twirling around her legs. She was wearing her shoes with the red soles, the high ones, that were impossible for kit to walk in. They were her going out shoes. Her fancy shoes. The shoes from her old life. "We have to celebrate!"

"We could go to Disneyland!" Kit knew she was shouting and she also remembered what Samara had said up on the roof, but this didn't count. It *couldn't* count. It was a lot of money. It was more than enough.

Kit's mom's expression changed and kit could see right away that she was wrong, that it didn't matter how much money it was, that Samara had been right.

"*Or* you could just pay off the guy at the color place," kit mumbled.

"What?"

"Nothing, Mom," kit said, quickly. "Let's go out for dinner tonight. Can we go to Dal's?"

"Oh!" Her mom pushed her hair behind her ears. She cleared her throat. "Tell you what, why don't you get us some takeout? I'd love Dal's. That sounds like perfect celebration food and just the right way to start spending some of this check."

"Let's *go* there." Kit knew she was pushing, but she couldn't stop herself. "It's not the same to eat it at home."

"Kit," said her mom. She picked up the dustpan full of hair clippings off the floor. "I can't."

Kit made herself take a deep breath. "Why not, Mom?"

"I'm too busy," her mom said. "I have clients all day and then I have to do paperwork. I'm sorry, not tonight."

"But we don't go *any* night. We haven't been for . . ." Kit squinted, trying to remember how long it had been. "Since last winter, Mom."

"Kit," her mom said. "Don't." Her voice was sharp. "Please stop."

"Can we at least eat it on the roof then?"

"Kit."

Kit shrugged. "Forget it. It's fine, Mom. I'll pick it up. But right now, I have to use the computer."

"Are you submitting your talent show form? I've had three reminders in my email this week."

"No!" kit called back as she made her way to the back room. She sat down at the computer. She could hear her mom on the phone out front, doing appointment reminders. She quickly Googled "forgiveness spells," which is what she knew Samara would have done. While she could still hear her mom talking, she clicked PRINT.

Back upstairs, she sorted through them. Most of them were silly (the eye of a toad! the tail of a newt!) but some of them looked real. She picked her favorite and then found a scrap of paper and wrote "naked mole rat." She searched through the junk drawer for a sewing needle and got a lemon from the fridge. Then she went out onto the fire escape. Spells worked better outside, she reasoned. The sky would have a better view of what she was doing that way and that felt important, although she wasn't sure why.

Kit sat down and swung her legs a few times, watching the people on the street below. Then she stuck the needle through the paper and into the lemon and she chanted nine times "I forgive you" while picturing Clem's face.

A crow flew down and landed on the rusty railing and stared at her, his head cocked to one side. "It's a lemon," she told him. She held the fruit under her nose and closed her eyes. It smelled fresh and clean and delicious, which was deceiving because lemon tasted terrible.

The thing was, she *was* a naked mole rat, so why was she even mad? Clem was right! But she knew the reason she was mad at Clem didn't have that much to do with the whole naked mole rat comment in the first place. Maybe she was sad because Clem wasn't Clem anymore, not the Clem she used to be. Maybe she was mad because *Clem* was always mad and being mad was contagious, like the flu. Maybe she was jealous because Clem was in a *phase* and she wasn't. Maybe she was hurt that Clem didn't seem to care about their inside jokes as much anymore, that Clem was leaving her behind.

Kit pulled her knees up to her chest and counted to twenty, hugging her legs.

At twenty, she took the needle out of the lemon and threw the fruit onto the roof of the hardware store. It bounced and rolled and stopped.

"Eat it!" she told the crow. "Then you won't get scurvy!"

She climbed back in through the window and took a deep breath of the plant-scented air. She put the needle away and then she picked up the phone. It was heavy, or at least it felt heavier than usual. She held it up to her ear and listened to the dial tone until the voice came on and said, "Please hang up and try your call again."

It must be a very old recording, kit thought. It had sounded the same for her whole life. She imagined the person who originally recorded it was young and glamorous like Clem's grandma in her old photos, but was now an old woman. She wondered if the old woman ever listened to the dial tone until her own, younger voice came on. In a way, it would be like her mom listening to her old record, hearing how she used to be before all of the rest of the things in her life had happened.

Kit dialed Clem's number. Mrs. G. answered and said that Clem and Jorge weren't home, and kit couldn't tell if it was the kind of "not home" that meant "they really aren't home" or the "not home" that meant, "They are here, but they don't want to talk to you."

"How *are* you, kit?" Mrs. G. asked, and she sounded so concerned that kit just knew that Clem had told her *something* had happened

Something bad.

"I'm *super* great!" she lied, and then she hung up without saying goodbye.

She went down to the computer in the salon office again.

"I thought you were done?" her mom called from up front. Her client was sitting under one of those big old-fashioned dryers. "That's only for homework, remember? I don't want your brain to turn to mush."

"It *is* homework," kit said. "I have to look up some facts about . . . flags." She had no idea why the word "flags" had popped into her head.

"No more than thirty minutes," her mom said. "What kind of flags?"

"Okay, thirty minutes," kit said, without answering the question.

The first thing she did was to check Clem's Pictasnap account, like she was looking for clues. *Kit Hardison, Private Eye,* she thought. Jackson wasn't the only kid with detective skills, but the difference was that kit would only use her skills for *good*.

Clem's Pictasnap featured a new photo of Forky sitting on a purple velvet seat that looked like it was in a theater. It was tagged *#forkinthecity*. And there was another new photo of Clem standing with a group of three people who were dressed up as dogs. That photo was tagged *#dogsofnewyork*.

Kit "liked" both posts. She never posted anything on her own account because she wasn't allowed to. Her mom thought that if she put pictures on social media, someone would see her and find her and kidnap her. She knew it was her mom's dinosaur brain talking and not reality, but kit certainly didn't want the man in the Batman mask to have any clues. She knew the Batman guy was real. She'd *seen* him. He for sure probably couldn't kidnap a kid, she reassured herself. He seemed to mostly just want or need small appliances.

She checked Jorge's Pictasnap, but there was nothing since the photo of Clem and his mom and dad outside the *TMTFIA* theater that he took before they went in to do the show. She had already "liked" it, a whole year ago.

Then she checked Jackson's. His account only had one picture on it. He did that all the time though, deleted everything except for one thing, so he would seem mysterious and aloof. This time, it was a photo of the letter he wrote to her with the purple pen. *It wasn't a lie!* It had fourteen likes.

Kit did not click "like," she just closed the window. Why would he share it with everyone? Was it a joke?

She opened Pictasnap again and before she could change her mind, she commented: "What do you want?" Then she closed it once more.

She wondered what he'd done with all the old pictures that used to be on his page, the ones he used to take of all four of them when they were still a constellation with four corners, a trapezoid of friends.

Then, just to make the lie she told to her mom true, she Googled "weirdest flag in the world." What came up was the Sicilian flag, which was a picture of a face with three legs coming out of it. Legs! She printed the flag out and left it on her mom's desk. She wrote at the top, "Weirdest Flag in the World, FYI (IMHO)." Her mom would laugh and then maybe she'd forget how upset she got before, about Disneyland and Dal's. Maybe they'd still be able to get takeout and celebrate, even if they just celebrated upstairs inside in the kitchen that was so full of plants there weren't many places to put plates anymore.

"I'm done, Mom!" she called.

Her mom waved. She didn't look upset, but it was hard to tell with her. She had a lot of practice hiding how she felt in front of clients.

Kit took the funny old access stairs across to the roof of the hardware store next door. The buildings had been built attached to each other, and no one else seemed to use these stairs for anything anymore. The staircase was a relic of another time. *Maybe they were built as a shortcut for the owners, to get back and forth to work,* kit thought.

There was no sign of the lemon on the roof, which meant that the crow had taken it. "You're welcome!" she yelled to no one. The crow was long gone. She wanted to laugh but laughing by herself just seemed bananas, so she swallowed the laugh back down.

She *really* missed Clem.

Then she heard a dog bark. She got up and carefully looked down over the edge. There, walking down the street, was Max.

Max was on a leash.

And on the other end of the leash was Jackson.

She blinked. "No *way,*" she whispered.

She took off her glasses and polished them on her shirt and then put them back on. It was unmistakably Max. It was definitely Jackson.

"YOU!" she shouted, but he didn't look up.

Kit made herself Samara-breathe.

Slowly.

In and out.

Out and in.

She swallowed hard so she wouldn't throw up. "I told you we should have let the dog out!" she remembered Jackson saying. He was such a *jerk*. He obviously didn't want to be her friend at all. What kind of friend would say *that*?

"K.i.t., keep it together," she reminded herself.

She watched Jackson bend over and say something into Max's ear. She saw Max sit and hold up his paw. She saw Jackson shake Max's paw and then give him a treat. Then Max started pulling on the leash. He was dragging Jackson down the street, away from his building. Jackson had to run to catch up.

"Max!" kit called, but Max and Jackson had disappeared.

She climbed back to her own building and went into the apartment. "Mom?" she called, but the apartment was still and quiet.

Kit went to the kitchen drawer and got out a purple pen and a piece of paper. She ripped the paper into small pieces. On the first one, she wrote, "I forgive you, Jackson."

“I don’t really,” she said out loud, “but I’m *trying.*”

On the next piece of paper, she wrote the same words again, for her Dad who was the Night Sky. Then on another one for John Alexander Findley, who used to date her mom when she was famous and then stopped when she wasn’t and was her father but now was dead. Then she did one for her mom, who sometimes did the wrong thing. And for Samara, who thought she knew kit’s mom better than kit did. She added one for Chandra, who wouldn’t let her take the naked mole rat. Finally, she did one for herself. That one was the hardest but felt the best. She doused all of them with Truth. *Maybe,* she thought, *making them smell like the truth will help to make them true.*

Finally, she scrunched each one up into a tiny ball and tossed it out the window.

She felt a lot better when she was done even though nothing was different, at least, not yet. It wasn’t even an official spell, she just made it up. But that didn’t matter. One thing she knew for sure was that just believing a thing was true was the magic that mattered most.

18 Clem

CLEM AND JORGE WERE AT THEIR GRANDMA'S APARTMENT AGAIN.

They were definitely old enough to be left by themselves, so it was insulting to Clem that every day, after school, when Mom was away and Dad was going to be at the store late, he had been saying, "Do you mind going to Grandma's from school to help her with ______?"

It all felt *contrived,* like they were being babysat without their knowledge.

"We mind," Clem had said today, but Jorge had interrupted.

"Of course we don't mind." He glared at her.

Today, the made-up reason for being there was that Grandma had said she needed their help to scrub her tiny balcony, to get it "ready for winter."

"Why does a balcony have to get ready for winter?" Clem complained. "Won't it just get dirty again? We'll have to clean it again in the spring."

"I don't mind," said Jorge. "It's kind of satisfying. I like this power washer." He sprayed it at a bird poop and the poop flew off like he'd hit it with a light saber. "Ka pow!"

"Have you been body-snatched? If so, say the code word." When they were little, they had seen a movie about alien body snatchers that had given them both nightmares for an entire summer. To make themselves feel better, they had come up with a code word that somehow they believed aliens wouldn't know. The code word was "pickle."

"Pickle," he said.

She threw a wet sponge at him. "Out, out alien!" She laughed but it felt fake, so she picked up the sponge and started half-heartedly wiping again.

Jorge was still laughing. He had been laughing a lot. Especially since his non-date date with Marina.

They had gone to the café across from One Buck Chuck while Clem had worked in the store, filling one hundred silver balloons with helium for a wedding. She actually thought she might die from the terrible smell of latex, but if she didn't do it, Jorge would have had to. Then he wouldn't have been able to go hang out with Marina. She was *trying* to be nice, to make up for how *not nice* she had been for what felt like a really long time.

Jorge had been gone for exactly forty-seven minutes, which was thirty-three balloons' worth of time.

That wasn't a *lot* of time.

It wasn't *enough* time for a person to change.

But when Jorge came back, he *seemed* different.

She couldn't say *how*, not exactly. His whole body moved with a different energy. He was holding a rolled up place mat. She didn't ask why, but he showed her anyway. It was a portrait that Marina had drawn of him, using a fat Sharpie. It was okay, but it wasn't, like, *excellent* or anything.

"That's great!" Clem forced herself to say, like she was Grandma admiring a picture in a magazine. Marina had drawn Jorge with a mermaid tail. "You're a merman now? She can't draw legs?"

"Hey," he'd said. "She likes what she likes. Mermaids"—he grinned—"and *me*."

"Hay is for horses."

"Hang on." Jorge disappeared down Aisle 5 and came back with a picture frame.

"You're *framing* it?" The balloons bounced against the ceiling above her, like they, too, couldn't believe what they were seeing.

"No! I mean, yes. Maybe. Why? Is that dumb?"

Clem gritted her teeth. "No," she'd lied.

He had shrugged and put the frame in his backpack, carefully writing it into the book under the register.

Clem scrubbed her grandma's deck harder.

She wanted to tell kit all about Marina and Jorge. She wanted to go with her to eat ice cream with colorful sprinkles. She wanted to lie on the roof and blow bubbles while they listened to kit's mom's record. She wanted everything to go back to normal.

"Whoa," said Jorge. "You're going to scrub the paint off."

"It's *concrete*. You can't scrub it off."

"Okay." He smiled.

What could have happened in forty-seven minutes that could possibly explain how *happy* he was?

Maybe Jorge said "I like you" and then Marina said

"I like you, too" and then they just did their own drawings and left and that was enough.

Maybe Jorge told her how Clem was acting lately. Maybe Marina reached over and took his hand or something and said, "It wasn't your fault," which is what Clem should have said but never had.

The mark left by the big flower pot wouldn't budge.

She glanced over at Jorge. She was about to say, "This is never going to come off!"

But Jorge smiled.

"Stop *doing* that," she said.

"I'm not doing *anything.*"

"You are, too," said Clem. "You're *smiling.* And stop waiting for me to ask, because I'm not going to."

"Okay, I'll tell you," said Jorge. He stood up and leaned on the balcony, like a romantic hero in a movie, looking moonily off into the distance. The wind blew his hair back. "She ate two cookies."

"You look like someone on the cover of an old-timey romance novel, like Grandma reads."

"I could only afford two cookies and two drinks, so I had to say that I didn't want one after she ordered two. I'm glad she ordered first. It was awkward. I drew her a picture of a dog. It was like the dog version of her. It was supposed to be funny. But she got super mad. She said, 'Do you think I'm a dog?' And I said, 'Dogs are the best!' and she said, 'So you think I'm the best but also a *dog*?' And I said, 'Oh, are you a cat person?' and I changed the ears to look more like a cat, in case cats were more complimentary. But then she was like, 'Now I'm a rabbit?'"

Clem giggled. "Oh, are you a cat person?" she repeated. She laughed harder.

"I know!"

"Okay, then what?"

"Then she drew me as a merman, and said, 'I have to go!' and she left. She gave me a high five."

Clem made a face. "A high five? Did she time-travel here from the 1980s?"

Jorge laughed.

"What did you *think* she was going to do? *Kiss* you?"

"I hadn't thought about the ending," Jorge admitted. "I don't even know now if she's mad about the dog drawing still or what."

"Always think about the ending." They were both laughing now and she didn't feel lonely at all.

She rubbed at her eyes. Her eyeliner left a big black streak on the back of her hand. It looked like she was leaking darkness.

Maybe she was.

Clem squeezed the sponge over the balcony. She hoped she didn't sprinkle dirty water on someone, but when she looked down, she didn't see anyone.

"After she left, I sort of hung out and talked to Jackson."

Clem was so startled, she threw the sponge at him. "Jackson isn't our friend anymore!"

"He's not *kit's* friend anymore. But neither are you. Do I have to unfriend you, too?"

"Yes!" Clem said. "I mean, I don't know." She scuffed her toe along the concrete and it made a satisfying bumpy sound. "He's been pretty mean to everyone all year."

"Yeah," said Jorge. "He had a bad year."

Clem wanted to ask what had happened, but she also didn't. Her loyalty was to kit. "Kit is a unicorn," she said.

"Really bad," said Jorge. "A really bad year. His dad left."

"I had a worse year."

"I know," said Jorge. "But I still talk to you. Even when you're a jerk."

"Good point," said Clem, accidentally letting go of the sponge.

"Hey!" someone yelled.

"Sorry!" she called down. She punched Jorge's arm, not too hard, but hard enough.

"What was *that* for?"

Clem went inside instead of answering. Answering was too hard.

19 kit

"TWO COOKIES, PLEASE," SAID KIT. SHE SMILED AT JACKSON SO she could telegraph to him that she had forgiven him. It felt good to be so magnanimous. The café smelled like some kind of pine-scented cleaner that made her nose feel clearer. She took a big breath in. "Actually, four cookies."

"*Four* cookies?" said Jackson.

She stared at him and tried to concentrate on nice, forgiving thoughts. He was still the same person he had been when they used to be friends, only now he had spotty skin and braces and he was wearing glasses, which were orange and perfectly round, framing his light-brown eyes. His eyes looked almost amber. They were interesting looking. She didn't know why she hadn't noticed them before.

"Do you want a drink with that? Hello? Kit?"

"What? Oh, no. Thank you."

"You're supposed to drink eight glasses of water a day." He leaned toward her. "The water is free." He pointed at the door of the café, where there was a bowl of water for people with dogs. Then he laughed.

"That's *really* not funny." Kit tried to remind herself she was forgiving him. She also wanted to know why he was being so mean. He was the one who had done the thing to her! Not the other way around.

"Why are you being like this?"

He shrugged. "I don't know. My therapist says it's a defense thing."

"I'm pretty sure that's victim blaming. I don't deserve to be treated the way you treat me. It's mean. But I don't want to talk about it, I'd just like the cookies." She paused. "You have a therapist?"

"I could give you a free soda. The thing is that four cookies with no drink is going to make you sick." He leaned even closer to her.

She could see the pores on his nose and a scattering of blackheads. She could feel herself blushing. The worst part about blushing when you have no hair is that your whole head can turn pink if it really gets going. She put her hand on her scalp, like that could stop the blush in its tracks.

"Why are you going red?"

"I'm not. Can I please just have the cookies?"

The person behind her in line cleared their throat. Kit didn't turn around, but she could feel their impatience coming off them in waves.

"Enjoy your four cookies," Jackson said. "Hydrate." Then, for no apparent reason, he flexed his muscle. He had a pretty muscular arm. It was like a teenager's arm and not like a noodley kid arm.

"Stop showing off and help the customers," his uncle said, coming up behind him. He put his arm around Jackson's neck. "You can't get good help these days." He shook his head. "Nice to see you," he said to kit. "You're one of Jackson's friends, right?"

"Yes," she said, to be polite.

"See ya, kit, my friend," Jackson said. "Enjoy your cookies and dehydration."

"You too," she said. "I mean enjoy your . . . muscle."

"What can I get you?" he was saying to the next customer. She hoped he hadn't heard her. "Enjoy your *muscle*?" Who said *that*? He would think he was making her nervous and that she liked him or something. She didn't *like* him. She was just trying not to *hate* him, which was even more exhausting than liking him would have been.

Kit took her bag of cookies and went outside.

Change happens both quickly and slowly, she reminded herself. It was possible that Jackson could change and be *less* of a jerk even. He'd changed into one, he could change back. That didn't seem impossible.

And, anyway, maybe *she* was the one who was changing. Maybe turning into a naked mole rat was like puberty.

Maybe it happened to everyone, they just didn't talk about it.

Maybe everyone turned into a different animal at various times, populating the city with a zoo full of inexplicable creatures who appeared and disappeared in a blink.

Maybe Jackson transformed when he was panicky, too, and whatever he transformed into was something lousy, like a cockroach or a dung beetle.

(She was lucky really. Naked mole rats were amazing and they didn't hurt anyone or anything. She grinned.)

Then, out of nowhere, she suddenly remembered something about Jackson's uncle.

She had been roller skating with Jorge in the park. This was last year. Clem was maybe still in the hospital. Jorge had been on his bike. He didn't like roller skates. They had been out at the lake where the swans were and then the weather shifted and it got cold and misty. A fog made it hard to see, so they were going home. They had just rounded a bend on the paved trail when, rising up out of the mist, they saw a tiger.

It wasn't imaginary, it was *real*.

The tiger was on a leash.

The leash was being held by a man who was wearing a long, black overcoat.

The man was Jackson's uncle, kit was sure of it.

"Whoa," Jorge had said, at the same time as kit was saying, "Is that a tiger?"

"Yes," Jackson's uncle had said, simply, as he passed in the fog.

But now when kit remembers the scene, she can imagine the tiger looking back at them, a grin spreading across his face in a specifically stretchy-lipped Jackson-y way.

"Not possible," she said out loud.

But she knew a lot of impossible things were possible. Coincidences and magic both could be true, even if it was unlikely.

"What if?" she whispered.

Why not?

Magic was magic was magic, after all.

Kit sat down at one of the outdoor tables. No one else was sitting out there. The summer that had seemed to hang on forever was suddenly downshifting into fall. There was a chill in the air. Kit shivered in her hoodie.

Turning into a tiger would be amazing. He was *lucky*, if that was his thing. Not that she'd ever ask. How would she bring that up? "Hey, I know I've been mad at you for a year, but have you ever been a tiger?"

Naked mole rats are way more heroic than tigers, they just don't get the same kind of press, she reminded herself. They were quietly heroic. They didn't have to be enormous and scary to get attention.

The tigers at the zoo had a whole enclosure called Tiger Mountain. There were big glass windows you could look through. Back in 2012, some guy jumped in somehow and one of the tigers had *eaten his foot right off.* Jackson couldn't be a *tiger.* He was not beautiful and he was not monstrous, just kind of dumb and hopeless about understanding other people's feelings.

But he had wrecked her life.

A tiger *would* do that.

Then it would pad away on its giant feet and take a nap.

The wind gusted and crinkled the paper on the bag of cookies. A few drops of rain splattered against the sidewalk, then a few more. She knew she should run across the street and give the cookies to Clem and Jorge but she didn't move. Three guys on bikes wearing skin-tight fluorescent outfits zoomed past.

"Go!" she instructed herself.

The door of the café opened and Jackson came out.

"I'm on my break." He was holding two hot chocolates. "I thought you might want one. Hydration!"

"Okay," she said. "It's cold out here."

"Why aren't you eating your cookies?"

"They're for my friends."

"So why are you sitting out here, freezing, and not taking cookies to your *friends*?"

"I'm not," she said.

"Okay," he said. He slurped his hot chocolate and then smacked his lips together

"Can I ask you something?" She took a sip, too, but the hot chocolate was too hot and it burned her mouth.

"What? I'm good at finding out answers. As you know," he said, meaningfully.

"I don't want you to find out answers. You should maybe wait until someone asks you a question." She liked that. It sounded exactly like what she meant, unlike a lot of the other things that came out of her mouth. She blew on her hot chocolate and a spiral of steam rose toward the sky. "I want to know why you say mean stuff, about me being a dog or . . . " She shrugged. "Why you say so much mean stuff at all."

He stared at her. "I already told you, my therapist says—"

"I didn't ask you to find my father," she interrupted. "I didn't know him or even want to know him. So why did you do that? I didn't ask you to do that. I didn't want to know that. I liked thinking that my dad was the Night Sky. I was happy. I didn't want my father to be John Alexander Findley. I didn't want to know he was dead."

Jackson leaned back in his chair. He put his hands behind his head, like he was relaxing, but she could see that his jaw was going up and down like he was chewing invisible gum or like he was upset and trying not to cry. "Sorry," he said. His voice cracked and then he swiped at his nose with the back of his hand. "My dad left."

Kit thought about how Clem's mom always said, "Hurt people hurt people."

She sort of got it, but she also didn't: Jackson lost his dad, so it was important to him that she lose her dad, too. *Fine.* But it was flat-out cruel, too. She didn't know what to do if he cried. Her hot chocolate was still too hot but she took a big gulp. She wasn't sure how to *get* it and be *mad* about it at the exact same time.

Neither of them said anything and the silence got bigger and more awkward. A few heavy drops of rain splatted on the table in a disappointed way. "You got tall," she said, finally.

He smiled. "I guess."

The door of the café opened and Jackson's uncle leaned out. "I don't pay you to sit around with your friends all day!"

"You don't actually pay me," said Jackson.

His uncle laughed. "Well, I give you a roof over your head."

"Yeah," said Jackson.

"Five minutes, Jackson."

"You live with him?" kit asked, when Jackson's uncle went back inside.

"Yeah, my dad left us and my mom sometimes is away at work so Uncle Jim lets me stay with him so I don't have to stay with my stepdad. He's, like, too busy with work, he says." He leaned onto his elbows on the table. "I kind of hate him."

"Oh." A lot had happened in Jackson's life that kit didn't know about. Somehow, in her imagination, he'd just been sitting across the street in his ugly apartment building, concocting plans to ruin other people's lives.

"Yeah, I mean, Dad just *left*. He didn't even say why, not really. Mom says he met someone else. He sends me an email every Sunday but it never says where he is or what he's doing. It's like he wants me to tell him all about how great my life is without being like, 'Oh, also, sorry I left and turned your life upside down!'"

"That's *terrible*," she said. "It's really terrible."

"Yeah," he said.

"Thanks for the hot chocolate."

"It was free, anyway."

"Do you know anything about tigers?"

His hand froze, his cup halfway to his mouth. "Like what?"

"I don't know, anything."

"Their pee smells like popcorn," he said. "Buttery popcorn."

His eyes met hers.

"Gross," she said.

Kit pulled open the door of One Buck Chuck. Jorge was sitting behind the counter, leaning on his elbow, sketching something. He looked up when she came in.

"Why were you sitting with Jackson? I thought you hated him. Are you friends again?"

"I brought you a cookie," said kit. "It's a 'sorry' cookie, basically."

"Thanks!" Jorge reached into the bag. "These cookies are the best. I forgive you. But what are you sorry for?"

Kit shrugged. "Things have been weird. I'm trying to un-weird-ify them."

"I don't think that's a word, but okay." He got off the stool and shook her free hand. "Consider it un-weird."

"Un-weird," she repeated. "But I think it got weird again when you shook my hand."

"I don't know why I did that!" He took a bite of the cookie.

"Is Clem here?"

Jorge tilted his head. "She's in the back. Balloon duty."

Kit made a face. "She hates the balloons."

"I know, but I have to finish this." Jorge pointed at his drawing tablet.

"What are you drawing?" Kit stood on tiptoes to look.

"It's for the talent show. It's my act." He turned the screen around so she could see it. It was a picture of a tennis racket. The tennis racket had an octopus crawling through it. "Is it too weird? I'm going to do a contortion thing."

"The talent show? Aren't you doing . . . " Kit made a gesture that was supposed to mean "acrobatics" but just looked like she was doing a chicken dance.

"What are you *doing*?" Jackson laughed.

"Nothing! I mean, what you usually do."

"Nope, not this year. We can't. Because of Clem."

"I don't know why I thought you would."

"I think a lot of people think that but we're not."

"Contortionist octopus, I like it." Kit didn't want him to ask her what she was doing for her act because she still didn't know. "I'm going to give this to Clem."

"Just to be clear, it's okay to be friends with Jackson?"

Kit shrugged. "I was mad at him, but I guess I'm not anymore."

Kit made her way between the tall shelves to the back room. She could see Clem, leaning back in her dad's big official Store Owner chair, her feet up on the desk. Mr. G. called it his throne. "King of One Buck Chuck!" he'd declared.

"Hi." Kit plopped herself down on the "visitor" chair, which was actually an inflated unicorn pool float. It squeaked. "I didn't fart. It was the unicorn. I have a riddle. Want to hear it?" She knew she was talking too fast, but she was nervous. "What did the unicorn call her dad?"

Clem shrugged.

"Popcorn!" Kit laughed. "Ba dum cha. Do you get it? Uni*corn*? Pop*corn*?"

Clem didn't smile.

"Why can't a T-rex clap?"

"I don't know."

"Because he's already extinct."

Clem shook her head. "Kit," she said. "Those are lame."

"I know. But Samara gave them to me. She thought they'd be a good act. For the talent show."

"You're doing *jokes*? Okay. Pretend I didn't say that."

"It's okay, I don't want to do them. I don't know what I'm going to do. Maybe I won't do anything. What are you going to do?"

Clem shrugged. "I don't know." She shook her head. "I *do* know, but it's a surprise."

"I brought you a cookie."

"Why?"

"I'm sorry. It's an apology cookie."

"But *I'm* the one who is a terrible person. I'm the one who said the thing I said. The mean stupid thing." Clem's eyes welled up.

Kit thought if she started to cry, it would look like her eyes were melting. "I know."

"I don't know what's been wrong with me."

"It's a phase," said kit.

Clem raised her eyebrows. "Maybe."

"Maybe Mercury is in retrograde," kit offered. "Mercury makes everything weird. So it's a phase *plus* Mercury. That can wreak havoc."

"How long are phases? How long does Mercury retrograde for? What does that even mean?"

"I don't know." Kit put her feet up on the desk. "Samara has a T-shirt that says BACK OFF, MERCURY IS IN RETROGRADE."

"Don't be a turtle." Clem sat up and reached into the bag. "These cookies are so good. Thanks. Want some?"

Kit shook her head and Clem put the cookie down and put another balloon on the nozzle and filled it up. "Tie this," she told kit, so kit took the twirling ribbon and tied it on to the balloon.

Things felt *better*, and sometimes better was close enough to being good enough for now.

20 kit

KIT PUSHED OPEN THE DOOR OF THE ANIMAL SHELTER AND THE bell rang in an upbeat series of chimes. "You fixed it!"

She closed the door and opened it again just to make sure.

When she walked in though, Chandra barely looked up.

"Hi," kit said.

"Look," said Chandra. "Before you say anything and get all hysterical and jump off a bridge or something—and we aren't in China, so no one will save you—that kid came back with his mom and they adopted Max. Max really liked him and I trust his judgement. *Plus,* that kid might be your sworn enemy or whatever, but he seemed like a nice kid. He has bad anxiety, his mom said. Actually, I almost couldn't get her to shut up. I know more about their whole miserable story than I should, believe me."

Kit sat down on one of the waiting room chairs. She was trying to decide how she felt.

"Hello? Are you going to say something?"

"I'm glad Max isn't dead," kit said, finally. She stood up and went behind the counter.

"You're not supposed to—"

"I know! Unofficial!"

"Oh, and guess *what*? I called the Bronx Zoo about that weird rat-thing."

"The naked mole rat?" Kit tried to keep her voice from squeaking.

"Yeah, that thing. Apparently one of their zookeeper's friends or roommates or something went bananas for some reason and kidnapped it and then it escaped. Who would kidnap a naked mole rat?"

"I guess it was easier to catch than, say, a tiger?"

"That's valid. Actually, it sounds like a good story line for a sitcom." She took out a piece of paper and started to write something.

"Are you writing a sitcom?"

"No, my grocery list."

"Oh. Anyway, naked mole rats are really cool. You know they can't get cancer? AND their skin is amazing. You can put acid on it and it won't burn."

"Who puts *acid* on a naked mole rat? When does that come up? What a world. Is there a lab somewhere where testers are dripping acid onto everything in the animal kingdom, just to see? I don't even think I'd be surprised. Humans are monstrous."

Kit shrugged. Then she smiled. Then she started to laugh.

"Why are you *laughing*?"

Kit's eyes started to leak. She was crying. "I don't know!" she managed to say.

"You're a weird kid," Chandra said. "You're a whole level of weird that is beyond weird. That's what I like about you."

The doorbell chime sounded.

Kit looked up. "Hey," Jackson said. "Want to come with me to walk Max? Chandra said you could show me some stuff he can do."

Kit glared at Chandra.

"What?" Chandra mouthed.

Kit shook her head. She picked up her skates. She went over to the white plastic waiting room chair and started to untie her shoes.

"Hurry up," said Jackson. "He's going to pull my arm right out of the socket." Max strained at his leash.

"Don't let him pull like that," kit said, standing up.

"You two have fun now, ya hear?" said Chandra, knocking her rings on the counter. "But no funny business."

"Gross," said kit.

"Whatever you say," said Chandra. She knocked her rings on the counter. Max barked. "Good boy."

"He always barks when someone knocks on the door," Jackson explained.

"I know," said kit. "I *know* him."

"Oh yeah."

All over the sidewalk, leaves lay in clumps, flattened by the pouring rain. Max pulled Jackson from one tree to the next. He was wagging his stubby little tail the whole time.

"He looks happy," kit said.

"Yeah, he's great," said Jackson. "So, like, not to be awkward or anything, but are we friends again?"

"Why do you *want* to be friends with me? You have . . . " She paused because she couldn't remember their names. "The Ethans. Ethan and Ethan."

The wind showered them with more wet leaves. "You know the leaves aren't really falling," Jackson said. "The tree basically throws them off."

"Really?" Kit was glad that she had stopped at home and picked up her real jacket, the puffy one that looked like a stack of tires. She pulled it closer around herself and peeled a leaf off one of her sleeves.

"Yeah, it's called *abscission*," Jackson said. "I'm very smart."

"I don't think smart people tell people they are smart." Then kit realized she still had the bag with the last cookie in her hand. She stopped rolling. "Hang on," she said, spinning around. "I forgot something." She skated fast back to the shelter and pulled open the door again. The *ding-dong-ding-dong* sound wasn't quite so charming this time. "Already, that's annoying," said Chandra, reading her mind. She looked up from her e-reader. "Why are you back?"

"I forgot that I brought you this." Kit slid the bag across the counter to Chandra. Out of the corner of her eye, she could see Jackson splaying against the glass like a starfish. He stuck his whole tongue on it and crossed his eyes.

"That kid is going to get botulism or something," Chandra observed. "I love these cookies, thanks."

"It's a 'sorry' cookie," said kit.

"Really? I thought they were just called chocolate chunkers or something."

"Nope, 'sorry' cookies. They are cookies you give to someone to say sorry."

"Well, that's *super* weird." Chandra shoved the whole cookie into her mouth. Crumbs fell onto her T-shirt. "Your friend is going to come right through the glass if you don't get out there. He *really* is starving for attention. He's needier than some of the dogs back there." As if on cue, a dog in the back room stared howling. "Keep your pants on, Chum! I'm coming."

"So you forgive me?"

"Sure. What for?"

Kit shrugged. "Making you late for your movie?"

Chandra raised her eyebrows. "I wasn't late."

"Really?"

The dog howled again.

"That one might be our new office dog. She's a sled dog. She took a serious wrong turn to end up here. I'm going to get her but you should really go before that one gets hurt. Or arrested." Chandra pointed at the glass. Jackson had turned around. He was pressing his rear end against the window.

"That is . . . not charming."

"He probably thinks it is," said Chandra. "What is he, twelve? Thirteen? That's some high quality teen boy humor right there."

Back outside, kit took the leash out of Jackson's hand.

"He'll pull you right over! He's strong. You're on roller skates!"

"It's okay, I've got him." Kit gave the leash a tug. "If you do this right when you first start walking, he gets that you're in charge. Watch this." She gave the leash a sharp upward tug and said, "SIT."

Max sat.

"Good boy." Kit watched Max's doggy face spread into a smile. "He smiles when you say that to him," she told Jackson.

"Really?" Jackson's freckles made the exact shape as the Big Dipper, across the center of his nose. She handed him the leash and Max stood up. "Try."

Jackson tugged the leash. "Sit?" he said.

Max sat.

"Good boy," Jackson said to Max.

"There. Now you've established that you're the boss, but you should say it like you mean it so he trusts you. You aren't *asking* him to sit. You're telling him." Kit took the leash back, even though she knew Max was Jackson's now, and Max started trotting along beside her, not pulling at all. "Not that it wasn't fun to watch him yanking your arm out."

"That's not very nice."

"Ha, takes one to know one."

"Want to race?"

"I'm on skates! You'll lose."

"Try me," he said, and he took off running.

"Go Max!" kit shouted, and they were off, tearing down the wet sidewalk, kit's roller skate wheels kicking up a fine mist.

Jackson stopped, doubled over, outside of Dal's. "Stitch," he gasped. "Stitch in my side!" If he hadn't stopped, he would have won. He was way ahead of her.

Kit tipped her skates forward so the brake stopped her. When she stopped, Max sat. "Good boy," she told him. "You have to tell him that all the time. He'll do anything if you tell him he's good."

"What a sucker. He should hold out for treats." Jackson was still hunched over. "This really hurts."

"I know a trick to make it stop hurting. It's, like, magic."

Jackson laughed.

"If you believe something will work, it works. That's science. Don't laugh."

"Okay, I'll try it. What is your magic spell?" He used finger quotes around *magic* and *spell*. Kit really hated people who did that. She almost didn't tell him, but then Max head-butted her leg.

"Fine," she said. "Promise you'll really try and not make fun of it?"

"I promise!"

"So what you do is you think about your pain," she said. She tried to sound calm like Samara.

"I *am* thinking about it," said Jackson. "It's not like I can think about anything else."

"Okay, great. Now this is the magic part: All you do, is . . . It's kind of simple. You just have to trust me."

"I *trust* you, okay?"

"Now imagine the pain going away, like it's leaking out of you. Picture it . . . like, *literally.*" The rain splashed into a puddle by their feet. "Imagine it filling up that puddle. And then in the space it leaves, imagine only warmth flowing in." She looked at him. His mouth twitched. "Close your eyes. Don't *laugh.* Just try it like you really believe it will work."

She watched while he closed his eyes. It was pretty tempting to stomp in the puddle and have it splash all over him, but it wouldn't have worked with her skates on anyway.

"Hey!" he said, opening his eyes. "That worked!"

"It did? Already? That's amazing!"

"I didn't know you were a witch. Just don't burn any pieces of paper with my name on them or anything."

Kit thought of all the paper she had ripped up with his name and how it hadn't changed anything. She wasn't allowed to use matches, so she couldn't burn them. Maybe that would have worked better.

"You already did, didn't you?"

"I didn't! I swear!"

"Then why are you doing that thing with your face that you do when you're lying?"

"I solemnly swear on all that is magic that I never burned paper with your name on it. Do you believe me now?"

Jackson raised his eyebrows. "I don't know," he said. "Maybe."

A man jogging ran around them. Then a woman on a bike chimed her bell. She was hunched over against the rain, her bright-yellow rain jacket ballooning up behind her. There was a cat in her basket. "BEEP BEEP!" she yelled, so they stepped aside. Max barked but he didn't chase the bike.

They both looked at Max. "Good boy," they said.

Jackson smiled. He grabbed Max's leash. "I have to go. Thanks for doing this. And for . . . you know."

It was raining so hard that the sidewalk was running with little rivers and she couldn't see very far in front of her. She started to slowly skate toward home.

The cars would have a hard time seeing in this downpour, so she didn't cross until there were a bunch of other people crossing at the same time. She didn't want a car to hit her and to make all the stuff her mom was scared of come true.

"Bye," kit said, but Jackson was long gone.

21 Clem

GRANDMA WAS IN THE BEDROOM, FOLDING PILES OF CLOTHES. She was going to miss the talent show because she was going on a cruise with Grandpa. "How does this look?" she asked Clem, holding a white dress up to herself.

"It looks like a wedding dress," said Clem, truthfully. She was supposed to be helping but she didn't know what "helping" really entailed. Mostly she was just watching Grandma try clothes on.

"I wore blue at my first wedding," said Grandma. "I wore yellow when I married Grandpa. Maybe it doesn't look like a wedding dress to me because I never wore a white one."

"Do you have a picture?" Clem asked. She meant of Grandma's wedding to Beau, but Grandma pointed at the big framed portrait of her and Grandpa on the wall by the bathroom door.

"I meant a picture of the blue dress," Clem said.

"Oh, that one. In the box!" Grandma laughed, like it wasn't sad that she didn't have it on the wall, framed, like the yellow-dress wedding.

"I'll go look. That dress looks nice on you. It will look really good when you get a tan on the ship. Maybe you could remarry Grandpa."

"Ooooh, good idea!" said Grandma. "The captain can do it."

"Take pictures," said Clem.

"It's stretchy!" her grandma called. "So I can eat all the food at the buffets!"

Clem went into the living room to retrieve the box from the shelf. Jorge was lying on the floor. The TV was showing old footage of a tornado in Oklahoma City. It wasn't even *current* news.

Grandpa was asleep. He slept so loudly it seemed impossible he'd be able to sleep through the sound of himself sleeping. The snoring was deafening. He would probably sleep through most of the cruise, but Grandma didn't seem to mind.

"Are you asleep?" Clem nudged Jorge with her foot. "What are you doing?"

"I'm resting my brain." He was holding perfectly still, like when they played statues when they were kids. He barely even moved his lips.

Clem got the basket of photos from the bookshelf. She tipped them over on the floor and started looking for one of Grandma in a blue dress. When she found it, it didn't look like a wedding dress at all, it looked like it was made from old jeans, all sewn together. She looked like a commercial for "Gee, Your Hair Smells Terrific." That was the actual name of an actual shampoo from the 1970s. Mom had found some at the Brooklyn Flea once and bought it for Grandma, because it used to be her favorite.

Clem glanced over at Jorge. He was still staring straight up, not looking at her. She slipped the photo into her pocket.

She didn't know why she did it.

Maybe she was a klepto, but just specifically for photos of her dead grandfather.

Maybe she was *cuckoo bananas*, just like him.

Or maybe, she thought, she just really liked the dress. She grinned. She had an idea. A great idea.

She went and got her backpack. She dug around in

it until she found the fork that she carried with her and then she tiptoed over and rested it on Grandpa's forehead. She took a photo to post on her Pictasnap. "Let sleeping forks lie," she captioned it.

Grandma came out. "Why does Grandpa have a fork on his face? Do you want me to walk you to the station?"

"Grandma, it is literally ten steps from the door of your building," said Jorge.

"We've got this," Clem assured her, grabbing the fork.

Grandma hugged them tight. "Stop growing up so fast! You're making me feel like I'm shrinking!"

"You *are* shrinking," said Jorge. "Old people shrink. It's to do with the fluid in your spinal cord drying up."

Grandma made a face. "I'm only sixty-eight!"

"Wellllll," said Jorge. Then, "Just kidding, Grandma. You don't look a day over fifty."

Clem rolled her eyes. "Love you, Grandma." She hugged her, properly this time, breathing in the sweet, lilac-y scent of her perfume. "You're my favorite old lady. I'm sorry you can't come to the talent show, but I'll get the video for you."

"Technology is amazing," said Grandma. "Thank you."

"Thank *you*," said Clem.

"What for?" asked Grandma.

"You'll see," said Clem. "It will be in the video."

At home, Clem and Jorge studied the photograph carefully. Grandma's dress was strapless. The sun was shining from behind her so that she looked like she was glowing. Their grandfather was wearing jeans and no shirt. It was a lot of denim.

"Why isn't he wearing a shirt?" asked Jorge.

"It was the 1970s! They were hippies."

"Still, he could have worn a shirt."

"Never mind his outfit, do you think we can make the dress?"

Jorge looked at her. "We can try."

"Thanks."

"You're welcome."

"I mean it, thank you."

"I know you mean it. You said thank you and I said you're welcome. Why is this getting weird?"

"Is it?"

"Isn't it?"

The twins stared at each other. "Are you seriously mad?" Clem asked. "I thought we were sort of kidding around."

Jorge shrugged. "I sometimes don't know if we are or if we aren't. You've been kind of . . . bananas."

"That's a stupid word."

"See what I mean? Like you get serious all of a sudden and then I can't tell what you want me to be, like if you just want to fight or if I'm supposed to laugh and it's sort of getting tiresome."

"Tiresome? For real? Gee, I'm sorry that my year of being mostly in pain has been so terrible for *you.*"

"Whatever, Clem."

"Whatever? Why are you whatevering me? You are the one who *dropped* me." She watched him flinch when her words landed. "Some days, everything hurts. Did you know that? Every part of me hurts. So I'm sorry if I'm in a bad mood! Ever! But I'm not even in a bad mood anymore, so now I'm not allowed to be happy?"

"But you *sneezed.*" He looked stunned. "*You* let go."

It was the first time Jorge had mentioned the sneeze.

It was the first time that Jorge actually said, out loud, in different words, but still: "It was your own fault."

Clem took a sharp breath in, which hurt, and clenched her fists. She opened her mouth to say something, but she didn't know what, so she closed it again and looked out the window instead. She felt terrible.

"I'm sorry," she whispered. Then she asked the question that had been giving her headaches for the whole year. "Do you think if they knew they would take back the money?"

Jorge stared at her. "What?"

"The money they paid us so that we wouldn't sue them. If I tell the truth, will they take it back?"

Jorge touched his face. "No," he said, like he was the authority on the subject. "They won't. They can't."

"Dad really loves the store."

"He does. And anyway, if you hadn't sneezed, maybe we would have won. We can't know. And you sneezed because of the dog, which wasn't your fault really. The people should have kept the dogs separately. The *show* should have."

"Okay."

"Don't look like that, they aren't going to take it back."

"I'm not looking like *anything*. I'm fine."

"Okay."

He looked like he was going to hug her. If he had, she would for sure have used her fists. But instead he reached into his bag and pulled out his sketchbook and his pen.

He started to draw.

She peeked over at what he was drawing. It was the dress.

"Pickle," she said.

"Don't be a turtle," he said. "Whatever that means."

On the morning of the talent show, Clem woke up with a really bad headache.

When her head hurt this badly, she had to move slowly, like she was moving through a swamp. The air felt thick and soupy and like it wasn't going into her lungs properly at all.

"You *are* breathing," she reminded herself. "It just doesn't feel like you are." She tried holding her breath. That was definitely worse, so she let it out and pretended she didn't mind that it felt like she was drowning.

She got out of bed slowly and walked over to the bathroom. She had stuck the two photographs of Beau on her mirror with sticky tape. She didn't know exactly why. Who wants their dead teenage grandfather looking at them while they pee?

"Avert your eyes," she told him. "I'm sorry you're dead. I sure wish you hadn't drunk that Kool-Aid."

Even though her head hurt like crazy, she felt good.

She felt good because she knew what she was going to do and it was going to fix things between her and kit, once and for all. It was her apology. It was bigger than a cookie. *And better,* she thought, but then she felt mean for thinking it. The cookie had been great. Anyway, *kit* had nothing to apologize for.

Kit was the unicorn.

Hanging on the shower rack was the dress that she and Jorge had made out of old jeans that she bought in a big bin at the Goodwill and washed in super hot water because Jorge said that if she didn't, she'd get scabies, which was a terrible thing to say and probably not true, but she didn't want to take the chance. She was itchy just thinking about it.

She'd cut all the jeans up and pinned them and Jorge had sewed them into the dress. He was really, really good at sewing, good enough that he could be on TV on a reality fashion show, and he'd probably win. She'd almost suggested it, but then she remembered about how terrible reality TV was when you were on it.

She watched the fabric race through the foot of the sewing machine while his fingers pulled it this way and that, like they knew exactly what to do. "How do you know how to *do* that?" she asked, and he just shrugged, like it was nothing. "It's not nothing," she added. "It's something."

"Shhh," he said. "I'm concentrating."

Her mom saw them working on the dress and said, "What are you making?"

Jorge told her, "Grandma's wedding dress" and Mom had laughed.

Her mom had so many different kinds of laughs. The laugh about the wedding dress meant, "I don't know why you're doing that but I think it's a lovely idea!"

Clem had laughed, too, and Jorge had looked up and said, "Why are you both *laughing*?" which had made them laugh harder. Then Clem had held up Forky and taken a picture for her Pictasnap. *#fashionfork*, she tagged it.

That was the fun part, Clem thought. And now it was time to get ready, to finally *wear* the dress, which was terrifying because it wasn't just wearing the dress. It was also singing the song. What had she gotten herself into? "Bananas," she said out loud. "This whole thing is bananas."

Then she made a face. "You dummy," she said. She stuck out her tongue at herself in the mirror.

"Sorry," she said to the photo of Beau, in case he thought that was directed at him. Then she laughed. "You're not even alive! Why am I apologizing to you?"

Clem flushed the toilet and then washed her hands and face and brushed her teeth. Her hair was extra curly, so she dunked her head under the tap, too, and the cold water made rivulets down her face when she stood up. She combed it as well as she could and patted it down. "Be good," she told it. Then she did two braids at the front like Grandma had in the picture. It felt important to do that. This wasn't just for kit, it was also for Beau even though he would never know about it. Obviously. He didn't even know she existed. Can dead people know things?

"Why'd you go and die? You missed all the good stuff, like watching your granddaughter—" she paused. "That's me, your granddaughter—watching me sing in the talent show."

Clem sat down on the counter. She had to decide how to do her makeup, either like Grandma in the photo or like herself. "Be yourself!" she said, sternly. "Everyone else is taken!" Then she fake laughed. They sold magnets in One Buck Chuck that said things like that. Dumb things that were meant to be inspirational. People loved them.

She could wear no makeup and be Old Clem. She could wear show makeup and be Acrobat Clem, like people would be expecting. Or she could put on her now-everyday eyeliner and be New Clem. Or she could do something different.

She leaned back against the wall.

Without makeup on, she looked pale and flimsy, like she wasn't all the way there, like the old photos of Beau that were faded by light and time. "We are both ghosts," she told him.

Clem took the dress down from the shower bar and put it on. Jorge had done a really good job. The dress fit her perfectly. She even looked a little like Grandma. Not Grandma *now*, in her white stretchy cruise dresses and wide-legged pants but Grandma *then*.

Grandma: The Denim Years.

Clem leaned closer to the mirror, and she started to put on her makeup. Her head was still aching, but it wasn't as bad. When she was done, she thought she looked good. She didn't look like Old Clem, who looked like Jorge, or New Clem, who wore too much eyeliner.

"Clem 2.0," she said.

She took out the vial of Good Luck potion that they still had leftover from *TMTFIA*. It hadn't worked that time, or maybe it had. She was lucky that she hadn't died. She was lucky she didn't break her neck. So maybe it had worked, after all.

She dabbed some on her wrist. It smelled really nice. It smelled like roses and ice cream and pancakes. It smelled exactly like what luck should smell like.

kit

KIT WAS ON THE FIRE ESCAPE.

She had gone up and down three times and she was getting winded. The last time, she peeled off the note about the TV. There were millions of TVs in Brooklyn for the Batman guy to steal. Why would he steal theirs?

Maybe that's why her mom always pictured bad things happening, she realized. By imagining them happening, she also stopped them from happening. But kit wasn't her mom. She didn't want to be her mom.

"I'm a naked mole rat!" she said. "I'm a superhero!" Which didn't feel quite true. It felt like she was trying to convince *herself* of it.

The rain had smudged the ink on the note and the paper was soggy. She crumpled it up in her hand and squeezed, then she climbed back into the apartment through the window and jumped down to the kitchen floor. The plants cast gray shadows on the floor that looked like dirt.

Kit was wearing her lucky hoodie and favorite jeans. She knew she should probably wear something fancy or different—maybe high heels like her mom was wearing on her album cover—but it seemed more important that she was wearing something comfortable.

Today was a big day.

It was the biggest day of her life so far.

Her heart beat faster, just thinking about it.

Kit put on her skates and then clunked down the stairs and swooped into the office. She checked Clem's Pictasnap and "liked" her picture of the *#fashionfork.*

Then she remembered what she'd been meaning to check. She Googled, "Does tiger pee smell like popcorn?"

Her mom came in. "What are you doing?"

The answer popped up on the screen. "Did you know that tiger pee smells like popcorn?"

"That is a *very* weird thing to Google," her mom said. "Listen, after the talent show, let's go to Dal's. We didn't do our celebration dinner the other night. Let's do it tonight."

"Really? *Go* there? Like . . . out?"

"Like *out*."

"Mom," said kit.

"What?"

"Nothing! Can we invite the Garcias?"

"Sure, why not?"

On her way out, Kit handed Samara the printout with the information for the talent show. "You'll walk over with Mom, right?"

Samara took the paper. She looked sad and thoughtful. "Oh, kit."

"It's fine if she can't or whatever! But she promised she would!"

Samara handed back the paper. She stepped closer and she cupped kit's face in her hands. "Kit," she said. "I love you like you are my own daughter. I will come to your show. But I can't promise for your mom. Remember what we talked about?"

Kit pushed Samara's hands away. "Mom *said* she'd come, so she'll come, okay? She told me she would."

She turned the computer off with her foot.

She didn't say goodbye.

She had just stomped up the stairs, Clem-style.

Maybe she was in the phase now, the mad phase, and she was going to be as loud as she needed to be.

If anyone got her mom, it was kit.

She *knew* her mom was going to try to come to the talent show, that something had changed to do with the song being on the radio and the money arriving in the mail.

Her mom was lighter again.

Happier again.

Everything was going to get *normal.*

Kit could tell.

What did Samara know?

It was just happening slowly, that's how change worked.

Kit was going to sing for her mom tonight, just like she knew her mom wanted her to.

She was going to show her mom that if she, kit, could be on stage, then being on stage wasn't scary and if being on stage wasn't scary, then being outside certainly wasn't anything to worry about either.

Kit liked how it made a full circle, how her mom's fears had started with her own stage fright and they would end with kit being on stage.

It was all going to work out perfectly, kit just *knew.* But she went into the bathroom and rubbed a few drops of Courage on her wrists, just in case.

Clem

CLEM BLINKED UNDER THE BRIGHT LIGHTS.

It felt like she had been standing there forever, even though it had only been a few seconds.

She could see kit waiting in the wings.

Clem was singing this song for kit.

The song was "Girls With Wings."

She took a deep breath.

The spotlights went off and then turned on again, illuminating only Clem. She tried to keep breathing.

She let the notes of the music start playing.

What if she forgot the words?

She smiled, even though it was the last thing that she felt like doing. She told herself if it really went wrong, maybe she could just move to Australia and start a cult of people who never ever had to sing on stage.

Then she heard her cue, and without thinking, she started to sing.

kit

KIT'S MOM DID NOT COME.

Kit watched Samara come into the auditorium, look around, and sit down.

This is not what is supposed to happen, kit thought.

She was distracted by her mom not being there, so it took her a second to realize that Clem was singing her mom's song.

How could Clem sing kit's mom's song without asking kit first?

What a jerk! kit thought. *What a selfish jerk!*

She might have said it out loud. She hoped she hadn't shouted it.

Clem sang the song so beautifully. She was singing it a thousand times better than kit could sing it.

The audience was totally silent, held still by Clem's powerful, magical voice.

Kit couldn't think what to do. She knew she was going to panic and she couldn't stop it from happening.

She listened to Clem's voice rising and falling and the words to her mom's song and she tried not to cry.

"K.i.t.," she reminded herself. "Keep It Together."

She pictured her mom's tattoo in her mind, the vines that wound around her mom's wrist. "It was a map that led me to you," she imagined her mom saying. "You saved me." But her mom was wrong. Kit hadn't saved her, she wasn't even *here*.

Her mom was good at saying stuff prettily like that, making it sound like a poem when really, it didn't mean *anything*.

Kit got off her seat where she was waiting for her turn to go on the stage and she walked around behind the curtain. Clem's voice rose and fell in all the right places. She didn't know what to do. She wished she hadn't come. She thought about leaving. Who would care? Who would *notice*?

Kit heard Clem stop singing and then the audience clapped loudly for a really long time. Someone shouted, "Bravo!" There was whistling.

Then Clem appeared, practically tumbling into kit's lap. "Did you hear it? It's the song of your mom's that we always used to sing!" She looked so flushed and *happy* that kit didn't know what to do with her anger.

She felt like Clem had stolen something that belonged to her.

"I *heard*," said kit. "It's *my* mom's song."

Clem hesitated. The smile fell off her face. "Are you mad? I mean, I did it for you. I thought you'd think . . . Sorry."

"*I* was going to sing it! Now I don't have an act!"

"What?"

"I don't feel good," kit said. "I have to go. Tell them I'm sick."

"Are you going to pass out?"

Kit squinted at Clem. She wanted to say something, she just didn't know what. She shook her head.

"You did a really good job," kit said. She could feel that she was starting to shake. Clem had sung the song so beautifully. Kit loved it and hated it in exactly equal amounts.

"It was supposed to be *for* you," said Clem. "If this was a movie, you'd cry and hug me."

Kit pulled her hood tight over her head. "I'm sick."

"You look like a turtle," said Clem, sitting next to her. "Don't be a turtle!"

"Funny," kit said, because actually laughing seemed impossible.

Mr. Hamish's voice crackled out of the speakers. "Up next, we have Kit Hardison."

"I thought you were going to do *riddles*," Clem said.

"I wanted it to be a surprise for my mom."

"Is she *here*?"

Kit shook her head. She was dizzy. *Oh no*, she thought. She tried to take deep, calming breaths but it wasn't working.

"It's supposed to happen slowly," she said.

"What is?" said Clem, from very far away.

Kit knew she was going to faint.

Or, more accurately, kit knew she *wasn't* going to faint.

Kit knew what was happening and it was much worse (and better) than fainting.

"Oh no," she said out loud.

She was smaller.

And then smaller.

She started to run.

"KIT!" Clem shouted.

But kit was already running.

Clem wouldn't understand, she *couldn't.*

Kit had to get home.

Her mom was at home.

Her mom would know what to do.

Her mom would understand.

Her mom would be able to save her.

That's how it was supposed to be anyway: Moms save their kids, not the other way around.

Clem

KIT LOOKED SUPER PALE AND SOMEHOW SMALLER THAN USUAL.

Clem couldn't figure out what her friend's face was doing.

"Are you *mad*?" she said. She'd meant for the song to be a thing. Something that was *their* thing. Like a non-turtle-y turtle. Like *all* of their things. "Did I mess up?"

It was like picking out a great gift for someone and spending all your money on it and having them ask you if you had the receipt so they could return it.

Mr. Banks poked his head around the corner. "You're up next, son." He was talking to kit, who didn't even seem to see him.

"She's a girl," said Clem.

"Huh?" said Mr. Banks.

"Never mind," said Clem. She rolled her eyes. "Are you going to pass out?" she asked kit.

Kit didn't answer. She was holding her hands over her ears and her face was all scrunched up. She said something that Clem didn't understand.

Clem had taken first aid—her parents made her and Jorge both do it for their twelfth birthday—and she tried to wrack her brain for what this might be. All she could think of was a stroke. "Hold out your hands!" she said.

Instead, kit weirdly dropped to all fours. "KIT!" Clem shouted. Dropping to all fours was not in her stroke training. "What are you doing?"

And then before Clem could figure out what was happening or what to do next, kit disappeared through the door that led outside. Clem turned around, looking for Jorge, but he wasn't there. "Jorge!" she yelled. She always thought better when he was with her to help her think. "JORGE!" She pushed open the door kit had gone through, nearly smacking right into Jackson.

"Where is kit?"

"She ran," Clem said. She felt out of breath. "Didn't she run right by you? I bet she went home."

"Is she sick?"

"I don't know! I don't think so, but maybe?"

"Hang on, I'm grabbing Max and then we can go check and see if she's ok."

He disappeared, then reappeared, dragging a gigantic black dog whose tongue was lolling crookedly out of his mouth, like it had been removed and put back in slightly the wrong place. He was beautiful.

Clem sneezed, three times in a row.

"This is Max."

"You have to keep him away from me," Clem said. "I'm allergic." Then she murmured "Good boy" to Max, just to see if kit was right about dogs smiling.

Max smiled.

"Come *on*!" said Jackson, who was already moving.

Clem realized that she was still standing there. Why wasn't she running? She took a big breath and started to run, faster and harder than she'd ever run before.

kit

THE WORLD STREAKED BY KIT LIKE LIGHTNING. CARS, BUSES, bikes, people, dogs, leaves, garbage, rats. She ran faster than ever and it seemed like it only took seconds and she was at the salon, running up the stairs over a giant empty Doritos bag, tumbling toward the entrance.

Kit ran straight up the door, her baggy-skinned hands gripping the glass. She went in through the mail slot, thumping to the floor, where she stopped, abruptly.

It took her a minute to adjust to what she was seeing.

Things were really blurry, but she could see enough to understand right away what was happening.

She saw:

Her mom.

The man wearing a Batman mask.

The orange record player.

Kit became aware of a sound, and that sound was screaming and the screaming was her mom and it was like the scene had been frozen and suddenly jumped back into the action. The man in the Batman mask stepped toward kit's mom and she stepped toward him, like they were going to dance, but kit knew this wasn't that. This was going to be a fight. Did her mom even know how to fight?

Kit wanted to scream at the man to STOP or GO or in any event to LEAVE, but naked mole rats may be superheroes who can run just as fast forward as they can backward, but they can't *shout.* So kit ran up the leg of the sink and into the sink and she grabbed the nozzle of the sprayer with her hideously long front teeth.

This is where I save you, she thought.

She sprayed the water at both her mom and the masked man. Then her mom, who was scared of rodents, even if the rodents were superheroes in disguise, screamed even more and the man in the Batman mask swore loudly and said, "This is just not worth it."

And then the door of the salon *crashed* open and in came Clem and Jackson and Max.

Big, giant Max.

Max seemed to *know* in the way that dogs always know.

In two seconds flat, he'd knocked the man in the Batman mask to the ground and was not going to let him get up, not for anything.

Kit blinked or fainted or fell and all of a sudden, she was herself again, full size, complete with rainbow star hoodie. She pushed her glasses up and everything came into focus. She got up from behind the sink and said, "Mom?"

Then her mom was there, all wrapped around her, her hair spilling over kit's shoulders, her lips against kit's skull. "Oh honey, I'm so sorry I missed your show," she said, like *that* was the most important thing right now.

Outside the salon, the lights of a police car flashed red and blue and red and blue.

"That all happened really fast," kit said, just as Samara came in. "I'm trying to figure out what happened."

"Kit?" Samara said. "You missed your own act! What happened *here*?"

Kit looked around at all the people, crowded into the small salon. "I guess I knew that I was kind of needed here," she said.

"You *saved* me," kit's mom told kit, and she held up her wrist. "I always knew you would."

. . .

Afterward, when everything had calmed back down again, kit had the idea that they could have the after-party on the roof of the hardware store.

They all took turns climbing down the metal staircase, even kit's mom. Kit could see that she was shaking a little bit, but she could also see how hard she was trying and how brave she was being. Jackson went next, and Max, and then Jackson's mom and his stepdad, Doug, even though he kept saying, "This staircase is almost certainly not up to code."

Kit could see why he might not be Jackson's favorite person.

The Garcias were next, Clem and Jorge and Mr. and Mrs. G.

Last, but not least, Samara, and then kit.

It was all of kit's favorite people.

The air was sharp and chilly. Kit could almost, but not quite, see clouds of her own breath.

After the burgers were gone, they talked about everything that had happened from the beginning, over and over, their voices layering over each other like leaves on the sidewalk.

Kit and Clem set up a blanket a little bit away from the group and they lay down on their backs.

"I didn't know you were going to sing," said Clem.

"You were really good," said kit. "I couldn't have sung it like that. It was good that *you* sang it. I can't even sing. If you weren't my best friend, I'd hate you for being able to sing like that. I'm sorry I had a panic attack and ran out."

"Is that what happened to you?"

"Yep."

"I didn't know you had those."

"Yeah, it's kind of new." Kit thought about telling Clem that the first time it happened was during *The Most Talented Family in America*, but she didn't want Clem to feel responsible. She wasn't. It wasn't anyone's fault. It was just the way kit was wired.

Kit heard Jackson whoop and then Max barked and Clem flinched. "I'm *really* allergic," she said.

"I know!"

"Kit, can I tell you something?"

"Sure." Kit looked up at the stars. They were really hard to see. They always were. She knew from summer camp that there were places, even not that far from the city, where you could see the stars so clearly, millions of them. There weren't fewer here, it's just that only the brightest ones were visible because of the city lights. *The supernovas,* kit supposed. Supernovas were stars that were dying, it's just that right before they died, they flared and became brighter than they'd ever been before.

Clem took a deep breath. "That night on the show, when I fell. It wasn't Jorge's fault. He didn't drop me."

"He didn't?"

"I sneezed. There was a dog backstage and I patted the dog and then I sneezed. I missed the part where I was supposed to catch his hand and I fell. It was my fault."

"I thought Jorge dropped you," said kit.

"Everyone thought that."

The silence pooled around them like water. *A puddle of silence,* kit thought. She could tell that Clem was waiting for her to say something.

"I'm sorry" was what she said.

"Why are you *sorry*? I'm the one who messed up. I patted the dog. I let everyone think Jorge dropped me. I might be a terrible person."

"I'm still sorry. It's not your fault you're allergic to dogs. You couldn't have known. You're definitely not a terrible person. And you're a good singer. A good singer and a non-terrible person. Pretty good combination."

"You're a really good friend," said Clem.

"Sometimes," said kit.

"Do you still think your father is, like, the sky?" said Clem.

Kit rolled over onto her stomach. She rested her head on her hands. "No. My father was a guy named John

Alexander Findley. He died a few years ago. Jackson found out. Jackson told me." Her voice was muffled because she was talking into her sleeve mostly.

"Jackson found him?"

"Yes."

"Is that why you were so mad at him?"

"Yes."

"That's a lot. Why didn't you tell me?"

Kit leaned up on her elbow. "I didn't want it to be real. I think it's like what you said about your grandfather and your grandpa. One is the one who made you but the other one raised you. The Night Sky can still be my dad. Right?"

Someone was playing kit's mom's record. She sat up. It wasn't a record. Her mom was singing.

"Listen!" kit said.

Clem sat up, too. Then she started to sing, too, really quietly.

Then other people joined in.

Kit couldn't tell for sure, but she thought that even Jackson was singing. Everyone appeared to know the words, which was weird but not that weird. The song was on the radio a *lot* now. But it seemed to kit like everyone was singing her mom's secrets, like all the things her mom was so scared of were being shared around somehow, and diluted by all the voices, making them less scary. That's how it felt, like all their friends were lifting something away.

Their voices got louder and louder and more and more powerful together and kit felt like her heart might actually explode. Tears ran down her face. She wasn't one hundred percent sure why she was crying. They weren't sad tears, but they weren't exactly happy tears either. Someone down on the street shouted, "ENCORE!"

Samara sat down next to kit after the song ended. She leaned over and gave her a hug. "That was amazing," she said.

"It totally was," said kit.

Clem laughed. "That felt like something in a movie!" She stood up. "Jorge!" she called. "Did you record that on your phone?"

When Clem walked away to find him, Samara rested her hand on kit's head for a second. "So what do you get when you cross a mole with a turtle?"

"I don't know!" Kit laughed.

"Why are you laughing already? You don't know the answer yet!"

"I don't know! I think because I'm happy. So what *do* you get when you cross a mole with a turtle? A mortle?"

"A tur-mol-eh!" Samara said. "Like a tamale, you get it?"

"That's *terrible.*" Kit stopped laughing. She groaned.

"It wasn't that bad!"

"I know, I'm just teasing," said kit.

Clem reappeared just then. She had bubbles.

"Where did you get those?"

"One Buck Chuck!" said Clem. "Dad brought them," she added. "He said he thought we might need them."

"One Buck Chuck is the greatest," said kit.

"Sort of," said Clem. "Except the balloons."

Kit stood up. They held the bubble wands up as high as they could and swung them. The bubbles were huge. The wind lifted them and carried them gently toward the edge of the roof, where they slowly sank down toward the street. Kit could imagine people down below smiling when the bubbles floated by them, like magic falling from the night sky, while they waited in the dark, in the sharp, cool October night for the buses that just kept coming to carry them home.

Then Jorge came over and grabbed the bubble wand from Clem.

"Hey!" she said.

"Pickle," he said.

He dipped the wand and held it up and slowly twirled. A huge bubble emerged and wobbled in the breeze, landing on Clem's head, like a lopsided halo. She got her fork ready. "Take a picture!" she said and she reached up and popped it while Jorge took a photo with his phone.

The night sky echoed with magic. From somewhere in the darkness, kit was pretty sure she heard a growl, and she thought she maybe smelled popcorn.

"What are you guys doing?" asked Jackson, coming out from behind the air conditioning vent, and then it was finally *normal* again. The four of them were talking and laughing, making a constellation of four stars, a trapezoid of friends. The bubbles floated on the wind. There was the sound of the adults' murmured conversation in the distance and the record playing on the orange record player, the rumble of the subway beneath the street, the sound of people's voices drifting up from the sidewalk, and the sound of the wind pushing a piece of paper across the roof—a note that had fallen out of kit's pocket—lifting it like a pale blue wing up into the sky where a single star was shining brightly, a spectacular ghost of itself flaring in the velvety blue darkness.

A Note from the Author

I'd like to talk a little bit about mental health, because even if it's not immediately obvious, that's a big part of what *Naked Mole Rat Saves the World* is about. It's about how anxiety can make you feel powerless. It's about how depression can make you feel like you are not yourself.

I don't know if you, Reader, struggle with anything like kit or kit's mom or Clem, but it's possible, even likely, that you or someone in your life does. It might help you to know that many people have anxiety or depression. Having anxiety is part of being human. Our built-in anxiety says, "I'm scared to be standing near the edge of this cliff in case I fall!" The other kind, the harder-to-explain kind, creeps around in the back corners of your mind and makes you feel scared, even if you may not be sure what, exactly, you're scared of. It might make you feel less lonely to know that depression can make us push people away, even while we wish they would come closer, and that being depressed is not the same thing as being sad, although being sad can be part of being depressed.

Sometimes our mental health affects our physical body: It can feel like a stomachache that happens only in math class, headaches that won't go away until you go home, chest pain and a racing heart that makes you feel like you're dying, or dizziness that stops you from participating in school or work or fun things just in case it happens when you're not in a "safe" place. This can shrink your world down to your block, your house, or even one apartment building, just like kit's mom in this story. Or it can show up like it does for kit, who gets dizzy and changes into something completely *not* herself (a naked mole rat!) in order to escape from stressful situations. Depression or low mood can make you feel like Clem sometimes feels: flat or angry or emotionless or disconnected or very much alone.

I was an anxious kid. My anxiety sometimes made me hyperventilate, which in turn made me faint. But if you'd asked me, I definitely wouldn't have known how to answer the question "Why are you so scared?" Mostly, I think, I was afraid of *being* afraid, but more than that, my brain was wired that way. It's how I was born.

If any of these feelings are familiar to you, know that you are not alone and what you are feeling is not your fault.

You don't have to have a reason to be anxious or depressed. Sometimes it can be triggered by something in your life (like with Clem), but sometimes there isn't a clear explanation for *why*. It just happens.

When kit gets anxious, she experiences a feeling of "fight or flight." Her option is *flight*. This is why she leaves school seven times before the end of September.

I know a girl who also experiences fight or flight, also usually when she's at school. When she needs to escape from a situation because her anxiety is ramping up, she would do anything to get out.

I know a boy with anxiety who suddenly, in an emergency, is the calmest person in the room. In situations where a lot of people would be afraid, he—an anxious kid—is not.

People with anxiety or depression are natural heroes and helpers. They are so strong because a person who has these things is also a person who is working very hard to overcome this invisible *something* all the time.

And all that internal strength helps them recognize when other people are hurting, and it helps them step up to help.

Guess what we call strong, helpful people?

Heroes, that's what.

Books and movies about fictional superheroes are often about people who were turned into heroes through some circumstance outside their control: a spider bite or an accident or an experiment gone wrong.

Anxiety and depression can give us superpowers, too: empathy, kindness, understanding. We may not look like heroes. We may not *feel* like heroes. But when we need to be, we can be.

I hope that you have a parent or a teacher or a friend or a neighbor in your life who you can talk to about what is going on with you. If you don't, there are some other ways to find help:

- Talk to your school's counselor.
- Visit **adaa.org** in the U.S. or **anxietycanada.com** in Canada.
- Call the Girls and Boys Town Hotline in the U.S. (**1-800-448-3000**) or the Kids Help Phone in Canada (**1-800-668-6868**).

- Call the Teen Line (**1-800-TLC-TEEN** or **1-800-852-8336**) in both the U.S. and Canada to talk to another teen who may have experienced similar feelings.
- The Crisis Text Line can be accessed by texting **HOME** in the U.S. to **741741** or in Canada to **686868**.

Heroes aren't just the people who run into burning buildings; they are also the people who listen, the people who share, the people who help, the people who are there for you, the people who care.

Maybe not now, but someday, that hero will be you.

Acknowledgments

A lot goes into writing a book, and a much larger number of people are involved than you might expect. I like to think of a book as a sculpture: As the first sculptor, I turn a lump of thoughts and ideas into a story-shaped object, but I have a lot of help refining that shape into defined paragraphs and chapters and then finally into a novel. So thank you to the entire team at Algonquin Books for getting out your sharp tools and making this book into what it is, right now, in this reader's hands. I am so grateful.